A Wretched Vengeance

Stephen K. Lynas

A Wretched Vengeance

Olympia Publishers
London

www.olympiapublishers.com
OLYMPIA PAPERBACK EDITION

A CIP catalogue record for this title is
available from the British Library.

ISBN: 978-1-80074-502-5

This is a work of fiction.
Names, characters, places and incidents originate from the writer's
imagination. Any resemblance to actual persons, living or dead, is
purely coincidental.

First Published in 2023

Olympia Publishers
Tallis House
2 Tallis Street
London
EC4Y 0AB

Printed in Great Britain

Dedication

To Cora, who insisted, and to Esme and Alex for always wanting more.

The Kitchen

In the bright, bright, much argued over kitchen, the sunlight lured in through the windows, turned warmer by the high coloured blinds, sparkled off crystals in the deep, dark green granite tops and bounced butter yellow off the beech doors and panels. It reflected everywhere from the stainless-steel appliances and the black glass of the oven doors and the graceful arc of the touch sensitive hob completing one corner. In those reflections, distorted copies of a young couple and their baby sat tied to the curved steel and beech chairs.

Aren't you supposed to want to die for your child? I thought.

'Choose!' the fat man said, finally losing his temper it seemed, leaning into Karine's face, sweat droplet running down his nose and a ripple running down his body, 'Him or it!' Pointing at the baby. There was a true menace radiating from him now and my time was up.

I had to force myself to speak before she did. I could see her lip trembling and her fearful glances around the room. I could see the sunlight glinting off her eye and a touch of sweat on her brow. Surely, I could save her. Save her from the guilt; but when it came down to it, I did not want to die! The child was not even a person yet! Six weeks did not a person make. Did it? All it did was yap and shit. It was still, in my eyes, a red-purple, wet thing, pulled from her womb after a very disturbing amount of cutting, snipping and tugging. Where was the bond, that supposed father-child love at first sight bond? Nowhere. Not in my head, nor in my heart.

In that paused moment it seemed to me that all those great heroic sacrifices of the past came down to a vague sense of duty. Of doing what was right. Of being unwilling to have people think ill of you, even though you'd be far too dead to care. It was not fair; and shit all to do with bravery. Christ! I was going to start blubbering like a child and it would be the last thing she saw of me.

I gazed over at her, tied to one of the lovely chairs in our lovely dream kitchen, and tried to convey that it was going to be all right. She was so beautiful and strong and full of energy and I felt myself so lucky to have had her in my life and as my wife. I caught her eye and was hoping to see love or despair or longing or grief, anything from her to bolster me, but all I saw was relief. She knew what I was going to say, and I felt the weight leave her.

I had one last look around this room that I'd come to love, just the perfect way the light hit everything and reflected, and how the colour changed from bright yellow to deep orange as the day aged. And the gorgeous smell, it always seemed as if a languid air brought in the scent of the garden which changed with the seasons and the blooms outside.

I was procrastinating.

'Kill me!' I said loudly, absurdly proud that my voice was firm. I couldn't look back at her. And though now in the greatest despair myself, I forced my head up.

The fat man shifted his gaze to me but stayed where he was. The little bit of his eyes that I could see were a very startling blue. Slivers of sky in the round pasty face sheened with sweat. The silver-streaked black hair was pulled into one of those ridiculous ponytails that I personally blame Midge Ure for, tightened up with an incongruous red hair-bobble. The white shirt stained with massive pit marks and a black lace tie dangling between moobs that were pushing double Ds hanging flaccidly over a ten pint a day beer gut.

I was about to die but wondered how the fuck a fat bastard like him got into the business. I could imagine him chunky and fit, eager to join and then building a reputation that survived his burgeoning obesity. Or was he always blobby, with a cold homicidal streak that endeared him to the thug fraternity, recruited for his apparent innocuousness maybe. Most probably though, as in all professions, it was about who you know. His blowsy mother, like a fragrant hippopotamus storming into bad Uncle Norm's speakeasy, 'You will give my Eunice a job in your little gang or else I shall speak to our mother!'

I could not even imagine how the hell he had survived school! Somehow though, he had managed it. He was now fully competent, big, bad and dangerous and he followed his gaze with his hand and pointed at me with the revolver.

'Looks awfully like your man is trying to be a hero, girlie,' he said in that strange voice. 'Perhaps we should let him. Eh? Take the strain, remove the pain. Eh?'

I tried for one last moment to catch her eye, but her head was bowed, and she seemed to be shaking and so, resigned to my fate croaked, my voice finally breaking with fear, 'Just fucking get on with it and shoot me!'

You laugh at the stupidity of people in films and TV dramas letting the baddies into their homes, aiding and abetting their own demise, but when it is you, it just seems a normal thing to do. The very large man with his brief case and his sober suit arrives at your door to talk to you about the visiting schedule for your new-born and you invite him right in. You do not think, nasty brutish thug has a gun and will kill you. Of course not. You bring him into your wonderful kitchen with the Chinese slate floor and island with an attached dinette table at which you point him, while offering to make tea and calling out to your newly budded partner to bring the baby because the man from the health service is here.

Perhaps though, something in my hind brain was firing. I still felt the pressure from the man's unpleasantly strong handshake and could still smell the somewhat floral aftershave sticking to my palm. A creeping shiver went up my spine at the strange harmonics in the voice. It was certainly one of those that did not fit the physical reality.

I turned to the sink to fill the kettle with water and saw him out of the corner of my eye setting his briefcase on the dinette and somewhat priggishly square it up and align it with the sides of the table. He then stood with his hands gripping the chair top and looked at the doorway.

Karine came in with the baby. She had that look that some women who have just given birth have. It's like motherhood has added to their aura, enhanced them at some deep fundamental level. She was practically leaking light and joy. She favoured me with her smile, and it warmed me to my toes.

Karine had decided on Poppy. I could not bring myself to call the baby Poppy, especially in my head. She said the name was ironic and that the child would grow to know that. My response was, at least internally, to wise the fuck up, because it was moronic and always would be.

I just knew that as the child aged, I would someday, perhaps at a moment of maximum embarrassment, let slip the name I'd known her by since she was born. Poopy it was and Poopy it would always be. Blame your mother I would have to say, she just wouldn't see sense.

She set Poppy down in her day cot on the table with those cooing noises that seem necessary to every action with babies and turned to smile at the man who had interrupted whatever mother-baby thing she had had going on upstairs.

Still unable to shake that strange discomfort, I also turned to ask if the man wanted sugar with his tea. He had taken his jacket off and put it over the seat back and now staring across at Karine he opened his briefcase and produced a large, matt black, oily looking gun.

'Please sit down,' he said, motioning with the pistol as he let go of the chair and moved towards the door.

'What the shit is this?' Karine said, completely calm. 'Why are you here? You've the wrong house sunshine? We're affiliated to nobody. Never were, never will be,' then she turned to look at me and unconsciously shuffled a little closer.

He had closed the kitchen door by backing into it, 'You!' pointing at me. 'Get the tie-wraps from my case and tie her wrists together.'

Taking my cue from my wife's recent response I shouted, 'No I won't. Just fuck off! and get the fuck out of my house!'

'Sher!' Karine cried, deciding to take things up a notch, 'take that gun from him and throw him the fuck out.'

'Of course, dear,' taken a little aback, I spluttered, sarcastically, 'I'll just ask the bad man to hold still while I gently ease the gun from his hand and then request that he turn around so that I can plant one on his arse. Shall I?'

'Dick!' she said, with some feeling, I thought unjustifiably.

We were just going to get into it with each other distracted from the reality of the situation, when I caught her eye and the slight nodding motion towards my highly expensive and most gorgeous Japanese steel knife set.

Just as I turned, hopefully nonchalantly, to grab the carving knife to use as a weapon, the fat man fired the pistol at the oven by the baby's head. The noise was immense, both from the shot and the crack as the ovenproof glass smashed and fell to the floor. Everyone was still for a moment as the noise slowly abated and dust cascaded down from overhead. Then the baby started crying.

'Ah, ah, aah!' said the fat man, letting a little steel into his voice. 'Sit down girlie. And you,' he added with venom, 'get the goat-fucking tie-wraps, put her arms through the gaps in the chair and tie her wrists together.' He hadn't moved from his position by the door, 'Do it now!' he shouted.

I still hesitated and as Karine started back towards the baby, the fat man fired again, this time into the bottom oven. The noise attacked our senses, swamping our ear drums, freezing us in our tracks like a baby rabbit in the headlights of the tractor just before it gets smeared all over the road. The wave of noise reverberated for a while, drowning out the baby.

'I just want to comfort her, you fat walrus, fish-honking turd!'

I always thought my Karine was brave, certainly braver than me. Others just thought she was bolshie. She certainly wasn't stopping. 'Look. I don't care who you are or why you're here, just stop being a fuckwit and let me get my child.'

The man smiled without opening his lips, a sort of upward movement only at the right-hand side of his mouth. I had read many times about killers with dead eyes, but this was my first, first-hand experience of such eyes and they were terrifying, that is apart from that strange waiter who once served me in Spain. Eyes deader than the fish he brought. Do they have partners, these people, lovers even, who look into those dead eyes whispering sweet little nothings? Empty, no emotion, no flicker of empathy. I could certainly imagine those unoccupied eyes watching as their hands dissected their own mother with a rusty, dull-edged carving knife.

'Leave it be, or the next bullet goes through its head. That nice little head will come clean off when it does,' the smile seemed to get wider but still no parting of the lips.

Karine hesitated and then slowly turned back to me and the chairs.

'Whale cunt!' she said to the man, as she sat down and pushed her arms backwards through the slats. She looked up at me, 'Make those tie-wraps too tight and you'll feel my teeth just when you're hoping for lips.'

I reached into the brief case on the table and took out a large black plastic tie-wrap. The reality of our situation suddenly hit me and made my legs wobble and my guts watery. I gently wound it around her wrists and pulled it as tight as I dared while feeling a small twinge in my groin. I squeezed her shoulders and bent to kiss her on the neck, 'It'll be okay,' I said, though with no idea how.

'Now you,' the man said, as he walked around behind me picking up a tie-wrap already threaded into a large loop. 'Sit down next to her and put your arms through.' I did as I was told while looking questioningly at Karine. Was that fear I saw? Not once in the whole time we'd been together had I seen fear in those eyes despite what we'd been through. The fear in mine must be obvious, though, I thought.

I looked back at him and shook my head, 'Listen mate. Just tell us what this is all about. No need for all this God-damned fuckery, and for God's sake let us see to the baby!'

The fat man looped the plastic loop over my wrists and

pulled it tight enough to bite into my skin. I gave a little moue of pain and watched as the man, moving around in front of us now, reached out and rocked the baby's cot till she quietened.

He then hunkered down until his eyes were level with Karine's and he stared at her for around half a minute, neither of them blinked, 'I have one, and only one question for you.'

I could see the sparkle return to her eyes as she jumped in, 'Yes! Yes, you are!' Surreal did not quite cover it. A man had imprisoned us and fired a gun in our home — twice. We should be shaking with fear with shit running down our legs but Karine was biting back. 'You are the fattest, sperm-whale fucking, stinking, sweat-riven, syphilis-ridden, hippopotamus's warty dick in the whole fucking miserable world!' she even managed a laugh.

The man had not taken his eyes off her, he waited for a few moments until he was sure that he had her attention, and he smiled that sort-of smile again and asked, quite softly, 'Which one shall I kill?'

Karine stammered to a stop somewhat taken aback. 'What?'

'You can choose,' he said, sounding quite reasonable. 'I will kill only one, but it must be your choice.' He waved the pistol slowly, back and forth between me and the baby. 'Your man or your little one. Your husband or your child. What's it to be?'

'Don't be fucking stupid, I'm not doing that. Fuck away off!'

'No choice means both. I'll give you thirty seconds,' he said, moving to stand between the baby and I. 'Come on now, which will it be?'

'You can't make me choose that. I won't,' I could hear desperation creeping into her voice. 'I won't. I will not. God. Sher!' she looked over at me, yearningly, I thought.

Your family tied up and you made powerless by another man

in front of your wife while he threatens to kill you all. Get out of this and nothing you do in your later life no matter how brave; no subsequent act of courage, no matter how extreme, will ever erase that all-encompassing sense of emasculation. You'll see it in her eyes when you least expect it, coming back to haunt you, that sense that you failed her, failed to protect her.

'Come on! Just fucking get on with it and shoot me!' I shouted again, voice growing stronger. 'Come on and shoot me! You fat bloated cunt! Shoot me!'

He came and stood over me, looking into my eyes now and, smiling that smile, continued to do so as he put the gun to Karine's head and pulled the trigger.

The noise was much more muted this time but the additional splat sound of parts of her lovely head hitting the wall made me vomit. I couldn't look but couldn't stop myself and will, to my dying day, wish that I hadn't.

Some freak of nature took that moment to have the setting sun appear below the window blind, and an angelic shaft of dark yellow sunshine appeared in the dust, still hanging in the air, and spot lit her face. Her head was bent to the left lying on her neck and even from this angle I could see that most of that side was missing, but it was her eyes, her beautiful eyes that looked so strange. The right eye was fixed straight ahead but her left eye had rolled up and was focused way out to the left, there was a drop of blood on her pupil and she wasn't blinking it away. I choked on my vomit and threw up again. The baby was screaming, and I saw the fat man calmly put his gun in his briefcase and snap it shut, lift his jacket from the chair and walk out, closing the door behind him.

I tried to lift the chair and shuffle over to Karine, but the leg caught on the grain of the tile floor and I toppled into her knocking her sideways onto the floor beneath me.

'Karine!' I said, my tears running down my face, 'Karine! No! No. No. Nooo!' My voice broke as I called out to the man, 'Come back, come back.' He didn't, and no one ever did.

The Church

My mother was a devout Presbyterian, a bigot and a hypocrite. My father pretended to be a Presbyterian for my mother's sake. A self-confessed bigot, 'Well isn't everyone,' he said, 'learned it at my father's knee and what was good enough for him is good enough for me, and of course, good enough for you.' I was thirteen, before I realised, he was being sarcastic, he hadn't a bigoted bone in his body.

His heart finally gave out after a lifetime spent in pain from wounds suffered in North Africa and Italy during the war. He was one of those that suffered in silence. This was just his lot, plenty of boys didn't make it back so he was lucky, was his philosophy.

I cried my heart out when he died and wanted to spend a few minutes with him alone in the hospital room to say goodbye. To say those things I never could to his face. It seemed that doing so to his body, with him gone, would afford me some sort of solace.

My mother gave me ten seconds and then came in and told me to get out, that the other people waiting — no family to me — had to see him too. Not sure I forgive that one either.

Their church, unusually for a Presbyterian church, was modernist-ish. A scallop shaped, smooth white plastered affair with the pews fanning out in two large blocks from a stage and a pulpit raised up, slightly to one side, in clear view of the congregation. The pews and matching panelling and the wainscotting in the corridors were pale oak and smelled slightly of the polish used that morning.

The women folk, grey widows all it seemed, appeared to enjoy the funeral arrangements and the day itself well, in the beginning anyhow. They seemed so much clones of each other that it was difficult to tell them apart without their hats on.

I, my mother, vague relatives and friends of my father and of the family, sat in the pews on the left-hand side nearest the pulpit. The right-hand side was empty, unless for a normal service or a wedding when it served the groom's family. It seemed empty at first glance but as I took my seat, I could see what looked like a girl slumped down on a pew, obviously asleep. She was wearing tight faded blue jeans, and a white T-shirt under a black leather motorcycle jacket and I could see clouds of black hair covering her face as she lay with her head resting on her arm.

The minister coughed gently to bring the flock to heel, did his welcoming bit and some prayers, then most of the other attendees sang the first hymn. I was always intrigued during prayers, to see who might also be tempting the high God of the Christians by not bowing their head nor closing their eyes. The fact that my father wasn't there — as normal — to catch my eye and grin raised a lump in my throat. This time there were no other risk takers it seemed. Dullards all.

The minister was well into his eulogy and I was thinking how much my father would have hated the bullshit being spouted about him. This man never knew hide nor hair of my father, even though he had been in this congregation for donkey's years. Oh! I know that they must put a little spin on it just to reinforce the message. That most important message to those faithful attending, that in Christ, life is eternal. I also accepted that I might be more concerned with my chances at eternal life when my knees would no longer keep my belly from the floor that I had just pissed on. But I doubted it.

The vicar was just finishing up — though I used to get my legs slapped for calling him that. 'Our church,' my mother would say with a wonderful pretentiousness — slap! 'Is the least pretentious of churches,' slap! 'No Papist gaudy tomfoolery or Dissenter vanity here,' slap! 'And our leaders must be addressed as minister only!' Slap!

He was doing a good job, professional, eyes tightly closed and voice rising in both tone and volume heading towards a crescendo, but I'll be dog-fucked if he didn't actually use the word! He called my father a saint! Saint! Saint Dad! I said to myself while hoping the daft clergy fuck-wit would catch the utter contempt in my gaze. I could hear my father laughing now that things had moved into the ridiculous — just as he liked.

Then came the minister's dramatic pause before his mournful 'Amen' and the girl farted. Loud, clear and resonant.

In that instant you could tell that huge thought, time and effort had gone into making the acoustics of the chamber perfect, because as things reverberated and slowly dissipated you could hear, against the mostly horrified silence, a large number of ladies sucking in their breath in disapproval while over them, distinctly, a little giggle and mumble from the same pew.

'Amen!' the minister said, obviously annoyed to have his well-rehearsed moment stolen.

After some shuffling amongst the congregation and for some reason dagger looks pointed my way, he exerted some self-control, coughed gently one more time and invited us all to sing the last hymn. Then, intoning in his best and deepest, most reassuring voice, 'Let us bow our heads and pray,' he moved unto his final blessing.

Once more, with absolutely exquisite timing as he paused before the 'Amen' she farted again, jerked upright, seemingly awake, said, 'You wee, fucking, dolphin-wanking, turd!' and slid back down softly snoring. I, all the children and most of the men, could not hold it in any longer and burst out laughing. The minister minced off the stage, took my mother's hand and they and her cronies filed out of the church to the hall next door, leaving the rest of us behind. My father would have approved, I could almost hear him clapping.

Of course, I had to pay the price for my disrespect. I was given a very humiliating and very public, dressing-down in full view of the other mourners and one thoroughly chapped off priest. It seemed that they had already passed sentence and they, like all petty people everywhere, needed to assign blame. As the adjudged catalyst for this unseemly behaviour in our Lord's house, I was dispatched to see to it that 'that girl' was kicked to the curb big time.

I wandered around the church perimeter, lacking a coat and shoulders hunched against the weather to find her sheltering, out of the wind, in the corner where the short corridor joining the church to the hall met the wall of the church. She was smoking a Marlborough cigarette and looked ridiculously cool and unattainable, lounging against a drainpipe, one long leg in tight blue faded denim crossed over the other.

She looked at me approaching and blew an errant jet-black hair from her face, 'Ah! So you're the sheriff then,' she said, with a small smile, 'come to run me out of town.'

''Fraid so,' I said, joining her by leaning on the wall as close as I dared. 'The grey ladies certainly don't want you around.' I paused and looked at her, trying very hard to just look into her eyes. 'It seems it's against the Lord's will or some such nonsense, you're being talked up into the spawn of Satan as we stand here,' and I stumbled over my next words as I met her gaze. 'Tell me,

Wha-wha-what was my dad to you?'

She blew out a cloud of smoke and with a hint of mischief in her eye, ground out her butt on the pristine tarmac with her very nice leather boot. 'Didn't know your dad. Sorry,' she pushed herself off the wall for a moment, uncrossed her legs and recrossed them the other way round and lent back again. 'I was coming home from a late night out, far too many vodka and cokes you'll guess, the wind and the rain were giving me hell and the door to the church was open. I sneaked in and lay down on the pew. I was just going to stay for a few minutes to warm up but must have fallen asleep.'

'Oh! Well look. I'd happily invite you in for tea and finger sandwiches or some of those disgusting tray bakes they make and gush over, but you know...'

'Tea! Thought it was a funeral!' She laughed, 'Do you not have enough drink to drown a battleship full of sailors in there for the wake?'

'No! No drink. God forbid! You have obviously never been to a Presbyterian funeral before. Tee-total, Temperance League stuff, you know. Not a drop of the devil's brew in sight,' I replied.

'You poor wee flat-fish fucker!' she laughed again. 'How can you stand it?' She moved off the wall and brushed past me making me feel very uncomfortable but in a nice hair rising on the back of the neck way. Her scent mixed with the smell of cigarette smoke gently grabbed me by the nose and punched its way into my brain. I had not until that moment smelled anything that intoxicatingly divine.

I pushed off the wall as well, turned to walk alongside her and breathed in through my nose as deeply as I could without seeming too obvious, 'I plan to ditch things here at the first opportunity, well as soon as we've done the cemetery bit, take my bike to the beach at Portavogie that my dad loved, and drink myself into a stupor,' I said. 'Then wake on the sand to the sound of the gulls and rage against the fact that she — my darling mother — won't let his ashes be scattered there.' Oh! No! much too reminiscent of those dirty, brutish, carnal pagan ceremonies.

'That's more like it. Jesus! If I ever turn into one of those mealy-mouthed, dried-up, self-righteous, own-sex flagellating, wasted old hags, shoot me with a shotgun full of spoons. No offence.' she added quickly, lightly touching me on the shoulder with one finger.

'None taken,' I said, then continued, 'I think my dad would have liked the way this turned out. With your sort of entrance disrupting the whole holier-than-thou thing.'

'I haven't a foggiest what you mean, but if I knew you a little better, I'd offer to come with you. Still. Bed awaits and the sleep of the dead for at least twenty-four hours, I think,' she said. And with that she started to stride off towards the large black iron gates that marked the entrance to the church grounds.

That bit — 'I'd offer to come with you' — did strange things to me and, as she walked away, I couldn't rid myself of the look in her lovely green eyes, her long black, slightly curly hair and her tight, tight jeans. The hairs on the back of my neck started to rise again as she turned around.

'Sorry about your dad, Sheriff. See you around!' She rounded the corner and was gone.

The Supermarket

Chief Inspector John-Henry McCracken had not the slightest interest in the religious nonsense that weighted his fellow RUC (Royal Ulster Constabulary) colleagues down. A boon, perhaps, in these changing times. He thought that he owed his success to hard work and grit but maybe it was political expediency. A safe seat — as it were. For he had no friends within the murderous orange gangs and was no friend of the green murderous gangs. He would happily shoot the lot and was not afraid to admit to himself in the safety of his own bed, that he had done just that with little provocation. An equal opportunity gun slinger, he laughed to himself.

Mainly, though, he had to live with putting them in jail. In jail! What a joke! In jail, those fucking H blocks, where they learned how to be a better class of murderous thug, taught by an old-guard glad to be tucked up safe and sound, with three square meals a day in better living conditions than they had in their terraces and tenements on the Falls or Shankill Road.

Taught the way of the bullet and the bomb, the way of the Armalite and the Gelignite. Taught fieldcraft and weapons handling all under the watchful eye of wardens and screws too frightened to do anything but turn keys.

Anyway, he shook off that old bugbear and brought to mind the latest. That toady, public school, pencil-dick of an Assistant Chief Constable, Martin James McClenaghan, had dumped on him, dumped on him from a great height.

On a lovely warm September morning in Rome, the Fisherman's ring had been wacked to bits with a hammer on the balcony overlooking St Peter's square. The papal apartments were now sealed, and the convocation of the cardinals was underway overseen by the Camerlengo. And this tiny part of the world was in uproar, because our own green son — Cardinal Jarlath Eoghan Diarmuid O'Bannon — was front and centre for the job of Christ's own high vicar.

Word had come down from the Papal Liaison Department to the Northern Ireland Office via the Foreign Office in London, that his Holiness's first trip, as soon as possible after the inauguration, would be to visit the old stomping ground and incite the papists to rebellion. Not that John-Henry cared. He thought that enough people voted with their wallets to make long term membership of the UK a certainty, and anyway, he would happily shoot thugs and 'terrorists' for a Dublin government as for a London one. He laughed to himself again, trying to imagine him or any of the RUC surviving a change of nationality.

ACC Fuckwit McClenaghan had accepted the job of securing said visit, against any fanatical orange bugger with the nerve to die for his beliefs and of course, since such public-school dickwads never actually did anything like real work, that meant him, John-Henry. Seconded for the duration on the ACC's recommendation.

So it was that all cases, and the chance to do violence in a fair and equitable manner to all types of scumbags and ne'er-do-wells, had been passed over in the interim while he assumed the guise of glorified gatekeeper.

He was already sick of the constant meetings with all and sundry interested parties and most especially sick of the Catholic

Church liaison group, and their unbearably pious ramblings about their new God to come.

It was in this good mood that he had been asked by his wife to stop at the supermarket and collect some asparagus, fillet steak and wine to complete her preparations for dinner with the Watsons tonight. He was also under strict instructions to source fresh oysters no matter what. Fresh oysters? He'd be bouncing all over town for the rest of the afternoon for those.

Pa Watson was a solicitor from Bangor, who seemed to specialise in conveyancing and would talk for hours about how the changing climate and worsening of sectarian violence was improving house prices in the suburbs. Ma Watson an ex-wedding planner from Dallas, was a petite blond with gorgeous curves, normally hidden, but usually on show at dinner parties, who had a thing for him. If he were drunk enough and able to brave his wife's evil looks, he would occasionally encourage it a little just to get a rise out of Pa Watson.

If he were drunk enough to do that though, he'd most probably start talking about the job and that would piss everyone off and lead to an early night but not the sort he was hoping for.

He got out of the unmarked he had borrowed from the compound and slammed the door as forcibly as he could, a learned habit. It just wasn't the same. Normally some, well disgruntled, constable would be forced into the passenger seat — can't have our boys riding around on their own, much too easy to target — and he could annoy them all day.

He just loved to pick the snotty ones that thought they were the shits after whizzing through the training college, and then keep them in the car like a hairy dog on a hot summer day while he did some trivial errands — can't open the windows on an up-armoured.

He used this a dipstick of quality. The ones that went crying about his breaking regs he never gave a thought to ever again. The ones that took the pain and kept shtum might be worth a look in a few years.

He walked across the car park, head on a swivel as always. A habit ingrained in him from twenty years on the job. God! He'd turn his bullet ridden, shattered body in his shallow grave if some snotty, slimy newbie RA earned his bones through John-Henry's inattention.

In the rest of the UK, the GB bit, there were supposedly chains of supermarkets, branches in every town, like bazars of old. Stocked to the brim with all manner of delights from the souk — well the continent. Here however, we had a local's best attempt — the Supermac. One hundred thousand square feet of prefab warehouse. Preened and primped on the inside and out, in an attempt to appear more than it was.

As he stepped through the automatic doors, he spotted a gaggle of shop assistants, some looking anxious and frightened, and a woman in a slightly different coloured uniform all talking at once and gesticulating. Sighing to himself and, wishing his wife had gotten off her fine, white wine drenched arse to shop herself, he approached the commotion.

He flashed his warrant card to the differently attired woman and asked if he could be of assistance. 'Thank God!' she cried. 'Quickly. Come with me.' She grabbed his hand and pulled him across a few aisles of high shelves stuffed with all manner of domestic goods, down one and turned right passed a shiny row of gut high, glass and steel cabinets filled with all the fruits of the sea. He tried to spy if there were any oysters on his way past.

'There!' she said, pointing. 'Sort that bugger before he wrecks the place.'

John-Henry now wished he could face down the belligerent shop assistant and return to the car to send the constable in, but since he hadn't had the good sense to bring one, he had to cave and sort the matter himself, much less noise that way in every respect he acknowledged.

A few yards away what looked like one of those homeless, street sleeping people was clawing at the milk products on the shelves, pulling them down on to the floor in seeming frustration. He was bedraggled and thin, drawn-out and wasted and was mumbling something to himself.

'Jesus,' John-Henry said to himself, 'this fucker's going to stink of old rum, vomit and shit.'

As he got closer, he waved away a woman shop assistant with a mop trying to get the man to stop. He paused for a few moments to assess the situation and then sighed and moved to come up behind the man to put him in an arm lock. There was absolutely no resistance and he heard the man say, sobbing, 'Breast milk! Breast milk! Get the Breast milk! Must be here! Must be here!' God! he did stink of shit, piss and vomit but funnily enough not of booze.

John-Henry grabbed his other thin arm and pushed it up his back as he forced the man into the shelf. It was only then that he saw a small bundle in the man's arm fall to the floor and as he looked, the cloth covering fell away to expose a partially decomposed and desiccated baby.

The Hospital

I came to myself lying on a bed in hospital. There was the usual paraphernalia around, about and in me, and the sounds, the beeping and the buzzing all seemed reassuring. I had a blissful few moments of complete blankness and then the memories fell on me like a ton of bricks and the pain returned. I lay there sobbing and shaking and groaning but the images would not go away. Karine was gone. What was I going to do with the baby on my own? Where was the baby? What had happened?

I started to shake more violently and shouted 'Nurse! Nurse!' A young nurse rushed in shushing me and telling me to be calm. Apparently, the police were waiting for me to come round and wanted to talk. She helped me to sit up and gave me some tablets and took my charts from the end of the bed and wrote some notes. She then left, turning her head and telling someone that I couldn't see that it was OK to go in as I was awake.

A tall, well beat-about, looking man in a dark well-worn suit came into the room and pulled up a chair by the bedside. 'Hello, I'm Chief Inspector McCracken, all right if I sit down and talk to you for a few minutes?' he said.

I had had no ID on me, but someone at the Supermac had recognised me as I was being dragged out and provided a name and a rough address. A car had been despatched to my house and found the door lying open and Karine's body. An official murder investigation had been instigated. I supposed someone had to tell me for some obscure formal reason, perhaps I was a suspect.

Murdered. Images in my head of noise and blood and bits of things and an unmoving eye with blood on it and a poor head in pieces.

I had to close my eyes for a few moments to gather myself and McCracken waited patiently for me.

Poppy was dead. She died of dehydration and I had no idea how painful that must have been for the wee thing. I felt an almost unbearable guilt over never learning to love her and had to turn my face to the wall as the Chief Inspector told me. He was not there to take my statement and wasn't going to be involved with the investigation but felt that he should be the one to break the news.

Apparently, I had broken free by breaking the chair back. Pounding it off the floor and my shoulder, which had been dislocated but now reset. My wrists were lacerated from the tie-wraps and there was a nasty gash where I had used a serrated edge to cut myself free from the plastic. I needed fluids and bedrest for seventy-two hours to set me right.

As he talked the memories returned.

His description seemed rather cold and matter of fact but lacked the aromas of the actual event, the mind-numbing horror, the panic at imminent death and the agonising thrashing around, trapped like a wild animal.

It did not have the periods of despair and tears, and the time when the baby's crying had me shouting at it to just, 'Shut the fuck up for a minute and let me think!' Worse, were those moments when I cursed the little thing, wishing it were dead instead of my Karine or simply wishing it were dead so I could have some quiet. Then the bouts of self-pity and guilt at suddenly getting what I had wanted, quiet. Then, wishing, pleading, even fucking praying that she would start crying again.

It did not have the shame of shitting and pissing yourself, the weeping and the raging, nor did it have the descent into the madness of dehydration and starvation.

Eight days. Eight days and on the edge of life I broke free. The flesh wants to survive I suppose, but I remembered nothing of my escape or my trip to the supermarket. Too far gone into my temporary insanity, brain dried out and dying, I had responded to some half-remembered instruction and made some feverish attempt at saving the child.

The Chief Inspector told me that the pathologist had performed the required autopsies and released the bodies to the funeral directors, Brown's in this case. The caskets would be prepared for me and a provisional appointment had been made at Roselawn cemetery five days from now, in time for my discharge. He would now leave me in peace and got up to go.

'You look like a man familiar with violence, Chief Inspector. A man capable of taking revenge just like in the movies, gunning down lackeys and hangers-on to get to the culprit and then killing him in the most ingenious way for sweet, glorious revenge,' I said quietly. He turned back to me.

'But what does a man like me do, I'm just a normal prick that hasn't been in a fight since school? What vengeance can I get? Whose blood can I spill? How am I to get justice?'

He didn't even answer me, he just walked away, and I went back to my nightmares.

The Bedroom

I love many aspects of this house that my father built, indeed I sometimes think that he reached inside my mind and pulled out those features that I would have included for myself. Perhaps my favourite was the Velux windows on the upper floor, placed such that you could centre your pillows under them and while lying cocooned and warm in your bed, look straight up at the most glorious night skies.

Karine and I were doing just that, her wrapped around me in that post-coital togetherness, warm, sated and comfortable with one another. We had ordered a large bed, bespoke and hard to get linen for, but we loved it, just a large divan with a Tempura mattress seven feet by seven feet.

It was a warm room, a terracotta-coloured deep pile carpet with three autumn pale-yellow walls that the sun bounced off as it moved throughout the day. The gable end windows looked out over the garden and the landscaping and shrubbery that I had worked on in secret to surprise her with. Where this ended, the view lifted to the nearby hills shrouded as always with early morning mists that swirled through the wooded slopes.

Each morning I bounced out of bed hoping to witness the morning sun shining through those mists, sometimes reduced to a painfully bright orange ball by their density and then as if at war, the sun's warmth would start to overcome it and the mist would dissipate, slowly at first then more swiftly until it was gone, and the sun shone alone in the sky in all her glory.

She stretched a little and then squirmed into a more comfortable position, then poked me to ensure that I was awake, 'Tell me the most embarrassing thing that has happened to you?' she said.

'What! Why?'

'Go on, just for me,' she pleaded in a faux sultry voice.

'Fuck's sake!' I said, 'The…'

'The things you do for sex, yes, I know. Now get on with it,' she jumped in rather impatiently I felt.

'It was in primary school, P6, and something in the cheap-shit paste that my mother had made my sandwiches with gave me diarrhoea big time. That fucking excuse for a teacher, Thompson, refused to let me go to the toilet. I mean who does that to a ten-year-old. I was squirming and closing my legs and biting my lip and sticking my hands up every minute, but he still would not budge. In the end, of course, the pressure told. I had almost made it to last bell and the rush to the bog, but it was not to be. He was in the middle of one of his rants about God knows what when I started to leak. It was quite quiet at first but as more people noticed he stopped talking just as the first of many, many eruptions started.

He was apoplectic, the cunt. Shouting about the state of his classroom and his floor — as if he ever cleaned an inch of it. He came as close to me as he dared without risking his hush puppy loafers in the mire and standing over me raised his arm and pointed at the door with the melodrama that we were all used to and told me to go home. He actually said 'Get thee gone' — dipstick. He even had the crassness to join in the laughter as I waddled from the room dripping shit all across his precious parquet.

I continued to drip and continued to erupt all the way to my house — a good half mile. I even had to stop and attempt to hide myself behind a car when I spotted two older young women, that I was normally most interested in.

They, initially worried about me, had the misfortune to come around and see if I was okay. Seeing me with my shitty pants down by my ankles and a pool of brown watery matter under my naked arse, they called me all sorts of names as if I choose to take a dump in the outdoors behind a Mini Cooper S every day.

'My onset of puberty fantasies about the bulges in their jumpers and curve of their hips and that mysterious lack of things at the top of their thighs often faded to nightmares involving large audiences watching me on the toilet. It's a wonder that I'm not damaged,' I said as I rearranged my pillow and pulled myself up to a more comfortable position and turned to the side to face her.

'No, no, no,' she laughed, 'you're definitely damaged. But in a nice way.' And she patted my naked arse, 'I want something juicy, with nakedness in it.'

'I'm beginning to worry about you, woman,' I replied.

The Top Gun Effect

Each year, in the autumn, the company I worked for held a conference in an English seaside town, usually in the same hotel that had just recently hosted the Conservative party — some quirk of the owners. This was the year 1986, and that year young men like me were giving thanks to the Gods of film for *Top Gun*, a film about an US Airforce Pilot and his paramour.

These events, by and large, were excuses to get drunk on the company's time and dime, and if you were lucky, to meet someone of your preferred sex from one of the other regional offices. Employees from all over the country attended and as air travel was banned due to the cost, my staff and I invariably ended up on the ferry overnight with hours of car travel at the other end.

Five young men on a weekend away and someone else footing the bill? The binge started the moment the bar opened on the boat. I was fortunate not to lose anyone overboard, because as you know in those days, you could spend the whole voyage on the outside of the ship with nothing between you and the cold dark sea but a four-foot-high metal rail. I was grateful just to be able to pour them into the car the next morning and must confess to being a little hung over myself. Completely irresponsible I know.

Luckily, this hotel had a pool, sauna and a masseuse and as soon as we got there, I availed of all three in that order and was restored for the night to come. A very strange thing having my first body massage, I was worried like all men I suppose that I'd embarrass myself with an inopportune erection.

'More an irritant than an embarrassment I'd say,' came the comment from beside me.

'Huh,'

'Your inopportune erections are more of an irritant than an embarrassment,' she elaborated.

'God. I'm so sorry. I'll endeavour to keep my unwanted, unasked for, in-opp-por-tune erections away from you in future then, shall I?'

'That would be nice. Now carry on,' she added, with that rather sensual smile she does when she wants to make me weak at the knees.

Although I tended to revile my own accent, many, indeed most, of the female staff from the mainland thought it cute. That advantage might be enough, but when coupled with the knowledge that I would be heading home the following day, far, far, away from anyone that knew them, it made me somewhat of a target.

'Oh! Sher talk to me, talk to me, whisper sweet nothings in my ear,' Karine laughed. 'A target?'

'I know, unbelievable, but wait.'

We had a sort of reputation to uphold. This was probably the third conference that I had been to and normally I would go with the boys from Dublin and of course the English considered us all big drinkers and expected no less — drinking through the night to breakfast — that sort of thing.

However, I been building my business and this year I had four of my own staff with me and they tried hard to push the boat out. I didn't quite mean to start things off, but Joe dared to suggest, while we were in the bar waiting for the festivities to begin, that I couldn't take my underwear off without removing my trousers.

Now I was still pretty flexible then…

'You still have your moments,' she interjects.

… and with a little straining, twisting and folding, I manage to get the pants off, thank God they were clean and just bog-standard boxers. By then I had quite an audience and I proceeded like some dumb high priest to sacrifice them in an ash tray while all hummed along with me like drugged natives from some dopey fifty's 'B' movie. I must say the management were very tolerant. Only coming up with a fire extinguisher when the knicks were well alight. I then retired to get new ones.

This goaded the boys on. We had Joe, who was a great dancer and liked hair against his chest.

'What?' she said.

'Jesus, this was 1986 everything had to be done in euphemisms, not that it's much better now. He liked balls on his chin.'

'Eh?'

'He bought his cucumbers as instruments of pleasure.'

'You mean he was queer?' she finally got it. 'Why didn't you just say so.'

He decided to crash a 'table full of squares' — his words — and chat up and proposition a 'gorgeous man' by telling him he'd never seen anyone more in need of a blow job — he insisted Robin Williams stole this from him for *Good Morning Vietnam*, unaware that the Vietnam War had been over for at least 10 years — and that he was just the man to do it, only to find out that the 'gorgeous man' was the group CEO and his wife was in the next seat across.

Eric managed to find his way onto the roof of the hotel where he proceeded to climb out along the flagpole and remove the hotel's flag. Five stories up. Fucking idiot, could have stayed on the roof and reeled it in, but legendary move.

The other two borrowed a car belonging to some guy who had driven up from London, a brand-new sporty white with red go faster stripes Ford Escort XR3i and crashed it into the first roundabout they came too, then ran away and left it there high and dry, like a model car on a wedding cake.

Of course, this was all to come after the drinking and my own next experience.

After the obligatory speeches had been suffered through, the serious drinking work got underway. I had the habit at that time of, once enough beer had been consumed, indulging in a few Southern Comforts. This inevitably made me sick, but I had been known to master that and return to the fray for more, many times. Glutton for punishment, foolish for sure.

The evening wore on with a bit of dancing and mingling and I was joined by one of the Welsh girls from the training school in Caldicot. She was a little older than me and married, I saw, but what did I care?

'You slimy wee, eel-fucking, bastard,' Karine said, poking me with her elbow.

'Look do you want me to tell you this or not. I'm more than glad to never say another word about it,' I replied.

'No, no. Christ! No. I want to hear all the spicy bits about how you wrecked someone's marriage.'

'She came to me! And anyway, I doubt that I was the proximal cause of that marriage breakdown.'

'Jesus! You and a married woman,' she laughed, 'and what has *Top Gun* got to do with it?'

'Ah! You remember the film. Tom Cruise meets Kelly McGillis in a bar, and he falls for her, sings that bloody song —

You've lost that loving feeling — and then, and this is the important bit, they meet in the loo and she sarcastically says…'

'Shall I just hop up here and we can just get to it!' Karine smiled as she jumped in with the line.

'Exactly. They never actually do anything in the film, at least in the toilet, but that scene planted an idea in many a woman's mind and as you know, young men couldn't care less if the woman he's with, on a temporary basis, is thinking she's Kelly McGillis going at it with wee Tom or not,' I said.

Well, the Welsh girl asks me what I would like to drink, and I say that I'd like a Southern Comfort, no ice, and then enjoy watching her walk away. After she brings it back, we drink and chat and she's doing all that touchy feely thing and laughing easily and ensuring that our thighs are touching and stuff. Then, she makes eye contact for a long time and she says that she needs the loo. I'm about to say that I'm not her mother, when it dawns on me. She leans close and whispers in my ear, "I'll be right behind you."

I can't say it was a dignified walk to the toilets because I was bent half over all the way there, with my jacket open trying to pull it down as far as it will go, trying to hide my bourgeoning tumescence.

'Bourgeoning tumescence!' Karine laughed. 'Your wee willie was sticking out like a carrot nose on a snowman.'

'It may have been,' I replied sheepishly.

Willie sticking out, half hidden by my stance but fooling no one who looked my way, I stumble to the loo. A quick look around, lovely, well maintained, bright chrome fixtures and acres of nice white tiles and no obvious obnoxious smells, just right for the planned assignation.

I check that there is no one at any of the urinals and that none of cubicle doors are locked, my luck was in. A few moments later she wafts in, puts her hands on my shoulders, gives me a quick peck on the lips, then pushes her underwear down her legs, steps out, reverses up onto the counter, hikes her skirt up over her hips, smiles coyly at me and opens her legs.

I push my trousers and pants to my ankles and worried that I might not last, decide I'd tickle the wee man in the rowing boat with my tongue.

'Fucking hell!' Karine has pushed the quilt down off her chest and is holding her stomach laughing. 'I haven't heard "wee man in a rowing boat" since I was 13!'

'You know! This isn't easy,' I said, slightly distracted by her jiggling boobs. 'Talking about this with you, I mean.'

'Sorry,' she said, mock seriously, 'you are doing fine, keep going.'

'Right! Where was I.'

I'm on my knees, suit jacket still on, trousers round my ankles, head buried between her legs. I haven't even touched her when a fierce cramp hits my stomach, and the Southern Comfort comes home to roost. I pull away quickly and turn, and in one hobbled jump, jump to the cubicle behind me. I push open the almost closed door and, knowing that I'm safe and the toilet bowl is beckoning, I release the dam and allow the vomit to hurl from me as I bend down to the porcelain. Unfortunately, there is already a head over the bowl. One of my junior, car-crash-in-waiting colleagues, is curled up hugging it, holding on for grim death, obviously in a rest period between evacuations.

As he turns his dripping head to look up at me, I catch, out of the corner of my eye, my Welsh date leaving in a hurry, seemingly mortified that her intimate scent has caused me to throw up. I don't even try to say anything, but as she is leaving, she has to push past my boss and my boss's boss coming in.

I have imagined, but never had the balls to ask, what went through their minds as they saw me standing over a young man with my semi-erect carrot just inches from his mouth which was, like mine, dripping vague white stuff.

'Oh! Fuck! Mother of Jesus. You poor wee fucker!' she gulped, trying but not succeeding in swallowing her laughter. Two seconds and she let it go, only stopping some minutes later with tears dripping down her face.

'I'm glad you told me that, and rest assured that not a bitch will remain untold.'

'You frigging asked me! You can't go around telling people my most intimate history just to embarrass me,' I almost begged.

'Your fundamental misunderstanding of certain terms of our relationship continues to amaze me,' she said. 'But I tell you what, to quote from your nemesis, *"Hey, Goose, you big stud! Take me to bed or lose me forever!"*' and rolled over on her back exposing all her lovely bits.

A while later with meteors flashing across the star filled sky above our heads, 'You don't speak of your family, very much?' she said quietly.

'You've some cheek. Not a word have I heard from you about yours,' I replied.

'Ahh but that's different,' she said, applying that sort of female logic that will be forever a foreign country to males. 'Go on — just a bit. I'm interested,' while, with a bit of instinctive psychology, moving her hand to the base of my stomach.

'Not much to tell,' I gave in, 'hated my mother, loved my father — no, not hated that's too strong. Disliked her many appalling attitudes. Hated the way she treated my father maybe. Hated the insanity of her prejudices, her controlling behaviours, the hypocrisies, just the constant stress of living with her. I had no idea how my father had coped for all those years until recently.' I paused and then let out the breath I didn't realise I'd been holding.

'Wow! It's as if I can feel the anger radiating off you,' she said. 'Breathe; let it go, relax.' She waited a few moments for my fists to unclench. Then, 'Didn't you say you had a brother?'

'He died.'

The Sporting Goods Store

Matthew was a rugby player and a good one too, captain of the school 1st XV and with the ambition, drive and talent to play for Ulster. He'd been good from the off, picked for every first team during his stay at school, and elected captain from under thirteen level all the way through to upper sixth. He fancied himself a singer and a ladies' man but was popular and well liked with only a little of that spiteful jock arrogance that made some sporty boys insufferable bullies.

He met a girl from the other side, she was a pupil at Aquinas Diocesan Grammar School, slim and dark, arts and drama, and a virtuoso with the cello. They had a few short months together before the storm broke.

Both her parents and our mother were adamant that things must end, each demanding that their offspring never see that 'Wee fucking Proddy bastard'/'Taig whore', ever again.

Tears and shouting matches followed but defying your parents openly just wasn't done. The bigoted adults were mollified when the young people seem to acquiesce but since when did anyone ever listen to their parents in matters of the heart? It was obvious to me that the lovers would ignore them. I could have told the grownups that but who would listen to me, I was only ten and recovering from a severe case of diarrhoea.

I never did find out how they met and even *that* they met was a bit of a strange thing back then. He started going to the youth club at the Diocese of Down and Connor complex, every Tuesday night at seven and Saturday afternoons once his game was over. This was held in some joined-up prefabs, shoehorned into the car park beside the Sisters of Mercy convent building. Five acres of 1890's red brick and sandstone buildings with manicured green spaces and well-thought-out plantings, including some plane trees that towered over the brick wall that surrounded things.

This youth club was looked after by one of those trendy young priests trying to connect with the young people by aping their mannerisms and likes, and by constantly playing their music on his omnipresent guitar, but with the *de rigueur* Christian twist. I suspect that it was only the presence of this priest that stopped Matthew getting his arse kicked-to-fuck and dumped in the street.

Maybe he slowly made friends or maybe he persisted because of her, but this became his weekly habit for nigh on six months before he brought her home to a mildly frosty reception that would have frozen a herd of bison. She then bit the bullet and took him home and he at least managed a few seconds in her hallway before her father suffered a conniption and pushed him out onto the street and slammed the door in his face.

Undoubtedly, it was that night that the riot act was read, ultimatums issued, and ignored. In two homes, far apart in a divided city, two teenagers plotted to continue their affair come what may.

Some weeks later, a miserable freezing wet October night with rain bouncing off the partially cobbled road ruined by the constant excavating of service contractors, he was on his way home from the club. He was most likely hailed by one of his friends. Maybe, 'You forgot your jumper.' Something innocent like that because he did not turn away to run. The single shot collapsed his right lung and took a piece out of his back the size of can lid. His 'friend' left him there to die on the pavement with his arm outstretched into the road and his blood running off into the rain filled gutter.

Sister Mary Josephine Immaculata O'Rourke was 99 years old and had been at her birthday party in the refectory that evening. She had gummed down some soft cake and the other sisters had shared in the harder cookies that had been sent in by a remaining nephew. 'Happy Birthday' had been sung to her in a beautiful harmony, which Sister Mary-Joe had thought the most wonderous gift and after Compline she walked slowly and painfully to her cell with its small, high window overlooking the street.

Serendipity, I would say, the Lord's will, the Sisters said, that just possibly the sound of the shot outside her window sent Sister Mary-Joe to her rest. Certainly, no one else seems to have heard it.

Mother Superior Ann-Marie Concepta Maguire stopped by to check on the birthday girl and discovered her dead. After a quick prayer she roused the other sisters and telephoned for the duty priest who was ensconced in the Parochial house a mile away, just settling down with a hefty glass of the 'water of life', a plate of champ and gravy, and the latest episode of *The Professionals*, which just happened to be his favourite TV programme.

After setting aside his tipple and snack he answered the phone, swore like a dockhand under his breath and said that he would be right there, Mother Superior. He grabbed his vestments and his car keys, climbed into the bottle green Morris Minor Traveller that served as the Parish's transport and practicing his 'Prayers at the Departure of the Soul', pulled out onto the rain-soaked road.

It would have been very hard to see through the rain splashed, fogged up windscreen but luck or the Lord was still

44

throwing sixes and the flash of Matthew's white jacket caught his attention. He pulled up quickly, jumped out of the car and knelt beside him in the blood on the wet pavement to feel for a pulse. After deciding that there was still life or the chance of life, he hitched up his robes and ran the 20 yards to the Sally port in the convent wall and pounded on the door.

Luck was still going Matthew's way because one the Sisters visiting had qualified as a doctor some years ago at Trinity College, Dublin. She was called to leave Sister O'Rourke's cooling corpse to go to the injured boy. To her credit she did not even stop for a raincoat or umbrella and it was that thirty to forty-five seconds that made the difference. Sister Brona Eloise O'Bannon, younger sister of soon to be Bishop Jarlath Eoghan Diarmuid O'Bannon, ripped off parts of her habit to stem the catastrophic loss of blood and kept his heart going with CPR until the paramedics could arrive and take over.

I remember the police coming to our house. My mother and father shooed me away, 'Go to your room!' and led the RUC Sergeant into the kitchen and offered him tea and sandwiches. I pretended to mount the stairs and immediately crept back down and put my ear up against the kitchen door.

'...lost a lot of blood, but thankfully amateurs. Single shot only — straight through, not like your Pro's double tap to the head,' he was saying as if offering comfort.

'Have you got transport to the Royal? Good. Well, I'll let you get to him and we'll come by and get statements and so on in a day or two.'

I ran for the stairs and heard the kitchen door then the front door open and close, some muffled tears it seemed and then the inevitable vicious, venomous sneering, 'It's all your fault!' from my mother, closely followed by a patient sigh from my father, not willing to get into anything, as he headed back to the kitchen.

They would not let me in to see him as I was deemed too

young, so on visiting days I was condemned to the car like a pet dog with the window cracked open and a bottle of water by my side. I'd be asleep by the time they got back. When I awoke and enquired, he was always, 'All right'.

Four weeks in the hospital after three days in intensive care and he came home. He seemed all right to me, but I heard the parents say that he was jumping at noises like a scared cat, flinching at the sound of TV gun shots and sick at the sight of blood. He refused to talk to them or me about it, no details, no suspicions, no reasons.

He also said that he did not recognise his attempted killer, but I could tell he was lying even if they could not. I was not at all sure of the benefit of not grassing on someone who, obviously not your friend, puts a .38 bullet through you in the hope of switching off your lights. Maybe he thought she would approve; I do not know. Anyway, the police caught no one.

Three weeks after coming home, he pipes up that he has found a Saturday job at the sports shop not two hundred yards down the road from where he was shot and within spitting distance of the old Youth Club. He let the parents rant for a while and then played his masterstroke. He was saving for a summer trip to Europe after his 'A' levels. And in case that wasn't enough, he needed to save for his Ulster coaching sessions before university. In the end they both thought a Saturday job would be a wonderful thing and even ventured to pay for his flights and his coaching. I smelled a rat.

I would be going to go to the same grammar school as him as soon as I passed my eleven plus. Not a doubt in my parent's minds nor any room for debate. So, in this context I had an excuse to visit the sports shop and browse the boots, shirts, shorts etc. that I would need come the following September.

I garnered a few quid from them to test the water with, so to speak, and headed off to the Ormeau Road the following

Saturday after lunch.

The shop was quite large, and it seemed that the owners had found a clientele ready and willing to spend their hard-earned cash on the latest legwarmers and newest chic sportswear brands. To help things along they only employed young good-looking staff. They then went against all the current building trends — small windows and large blank walls, the better to weather bomb explosions — in having huge windows so that all and sundry could get a good look at the stock and the staff.

It was a bright place, posters of fit and beautiful men and women on the walls wearing the most up to date gear. The music was turned up too loud — in my view — and they even went so far as to have carpeted floors and a sitting area for people to discuss what sports clothes they were going to buy, I suppose. Although it was probably an excuse to rest and ogle the young and tender legitimately.

I was browsing the rugby shirts and looking around for someone to show me the matching shorts and it wasn't really a surprise, when I was approached by a young girl asking if she could help, to recognise her as the paramour *Catholique*.

They say love is blind, but Matthew's must have been blind, deaf and dumb to think that his friendly shooter was going to just let this go. A woman was at stake.

A man might share his hearth and home with you. He might share his last morsel of bread or mouthful of water. He might even risk his life to preserve yours, but as soon as your kind touch his womenfolk the Klan comes out, the hoods go on and the fire is put to the cross.

I'm no Sherlock Holmes but it took me less than a second to guess the score and that was just after he was shot. On the other hand, the police were useless. Oh! I know that they were too busy teeing up members of the Provo's and Sinn Fein's families to murderous 'Loyalist' scum to bother much with a proper investigation, but still. Wasn't it obvious? Some jealous motherfucker with connections to the IRA fancied the babe and didn't want any dirty Proddy hands on her. And having failed once I suppose our unrequited homicidal toe-rag decided that if he couldn't have her no one shall.

Matthew and his *coeur d'amour* were both on the evening shift at the shop, no doubt relishing their time together and feeling good about having pulled a fast one on the parents.

Around closing up time, something was jammed under the front door lever and a gallon can of petrol laced with Vaseline and a half pound of Semtex was hung on the security grill covering the window on the top half.

I have this recurring vision of the toe-rag knocking on the door to attract their attention then running away laughing as they approach, only to walk into the explosion. Both were found at the front door, curled up, burnt into a single mass of flesh such that it was impossible to separate one from the other.

I was quiet for a while and Karine just breathed softly beside me. Then she said 'God! I'm so sorry, do you still miss him?'

'Not really,' I replied, 'I couldn't seem to feel anything at the time and still don't. Perhaps it's because he forced me to wank him off so many times.'

Five beats of my heart. 'By the way, I love you and want you to be my wife.'

In a rather smaller voice than I had hoped, she said 'Okay.'

The Funeral

I looked down the hill to the city spread out below and just visible through the fine misty rain. I had been standing there for a long time. I'd stood there while they had held the service — non-denominational. I'd stood there, all through the parade of 'sorry for your loss's', and the hugs, sincere and otherwise, from well-wishers, obviously wondering why I had not attended and spoken at the service in the little chapel at the crematorium attached to the cemetery. I'd stood there ignoring the moans of the council workers trying to work around me, while the coffins were brought from the stands inside and lowered into the ground. I'd stood there through the last prayers and comments from some vicar allied to the council, on remittance no doubt, who knew not the slightest thing about her. I had stood there as the people faded away and left me in peace.

It was rather beautiful this place. The paths were laid in concentric rows climbing the small hills. In the valleys and creases were small stands of trees and shrubs holding quiet places with benches. All those that I could see had plaques affixed with dedications to loved ones passed. Surrounding the large cemetery area were many more trees, these to feed the latest trend of pouring out your deceased's ashes at the base of something that would take them up and grow. Many of these trees held wreaths, bundles of flowers and even small toys and teddies. I was surprised to see a uniformed worker walking among the trees removing these. No doubt some ridiculous regulation of the council, arrived at with all the feeling committees give to every decision they make.

I would occasionally look at the grave in front of me, still open, that bore those two coffins, one tiny white one and one large mahogany one. She had not wanted to be burnt and I had taken no comfort in the well-meaning 'at least they'll be together' noises. My tears ran down my face and joined the raindrops falling on to my shoes and I had decided that I'd stand there forever.

A soft cough disturbed me, I turned my head, 'Chief Inspector?' I said, somewhat surprised.

'I know it's often meaningless, but you have my condolences nonetheless,' he said, as he came to stand beside me. 'I waited to see you in the car park but thought I'd try here before giving up,' he added.

'See me? Do you have news?' I asked, a desperate hope leaking into my voice.

'No. I'm sorry. As you know I'm not involved directly in the case but I'm sure that the folk concerned will keep you up to speed on any developments.'

I was silent a moment and disappointed, turned from him to gaze out over the city again and then as if he had remembered my question from the hospital.

'I know. It's never enough; but it's all we've got. We'll find the man responsible and we'll put him behind bars for the rest of his life,' he said. 'It won't feel like justice because they are dead,' nodding towards the grave, 'and he will get to carry on living.'

'Then what's the point,' I sighed. 'It will never be justice for me to know that my wife's killer languishes in prison, eating well, perhaps getting an education so that he can impress the probation board and escape to the world after ten or fifteen years.'

I looked back into the wet dirty hole in the ground that my sparkling, effervescent woman and our little daughter had been committed to.

'I was never one for capital punishment. I could never see how the state had the right to take a life. The state can't hate or feel a need for vengeance, can't dream about making a human suffer for his acts. These are things left to us untimely bereaved and now I'm one of those. Left to come to terms with jail equals justice,' I scuffed at the wet sticky mud at my feet.

'Your colleague — can't even remember his name — the Chief Inspector on the case, has told me they've gotten nowhere anyway, and I sit staring at the walls dreaming of hurting people — as if I could.'

We were both silent again for a few seconds turned to look over the city. The first few lights were coming on to dispel the late autumn gloom and the greyness of the weather. All those families tucked up warm and safe in their homes, sharing their day's activities over dinner, perhaps planning a cosy night in with wine and romance. Self-pity mixed with grief and despair made me cough a little to stop from crying again and I think he took this as his queue to leave.

'Look, I'm not supposed to comment on these things, but an awful lot of stuff is being set back by this upcoming visit of the Holy Father elect. I'm sure that things will start happening once all that is over, and things get back to normal,' he said.

'I need to do something, anything! I need *her* to feel that I am,' I said, pointing at the coffin. 'Not that she can of course — fucking ridiculous.' I paused then carried on. 'Isn't there anything you can tell me?' I hated myself for pleading.

He went quiet, and stared at his shoes for a long moment, then he seemed to come to a decision and lifted his head, 'I overheard your Chief Inspector talking of an aborted raid on a creep who owns/runs — don't know — a bar near the docks called the Sailor's Rest,' he said. 'I don't know how that, or if that, will help, but it's all I've got.'

'You'd be surprised how much knowing something concrete, even if it turns out to be nothing, works. It's like you suddenly have an anchor after being tossed about in a storm at sea,' I replied, a sudden energy in my voice.

He shrugged his shoulders and shook my hand, 'Well, I don't know about that but look after yourself,' and turned and walked away.

The Pound Music Club

Little in the way of entertainment venues managed to stay open in those dreary, dark days. They failed because they would not pay protection and were firebombed, or were closed because they had turned into free-for-all, blood-spurting, riotous circuses. Mostly though, they closed through fear. Who, in their right mind, would risk death and damnation for a disco or a dance, or risk a bullet or a bomb to see a band? As it turns out we would. The young. With nothing else to spend our money on and graced with the inability to perceive our own mortality.

This was a time for fuck's sake, when public pools and parks, cinemas and pubs had to close on a Sunday — God's Presbyterian day! This was a time when the city centre was ringed with steel gates, manned by civilian searchers, who went through your shopping bags and gave you a pat down before you could visit the likes of C&A and British Home Stores.

This was also the heyday of the Pound Music Club.

A small narrow, not terribly clean place nestled in a back street between the Law Courts and the main bus terminus, the Pound Music Club provided a rock music haven. A light in the darkness, where a local band led by a virtuoso of the guitar, one Jim Armstrong, and his crew, would give us covers of Led Zeppelin's 'Stairway to Heaven' and Lynyrd Skynyrd's 'Free Bird'. They would transport us, for an afternoon, to open air concerts with thousands of people listening and living in peace and freedom. The band would always finish with a local boy's song — Van Morrison's 'Gloria' — which we would sing at the top of our voices. Then we would stumble, half-blinded, sated and deafened, into the street where we would pick up our bikes and roar home to our local for an evening's drinking.

It was not that the drink driving laws were liberal, it was just that the Boys had other things on their minds most of the time, and thus Saturday afternoons became something to long for and to live for.

The Saturday after my father's funeral, a bright day in March, when I was just about to hit my mother with a garden spade, the doorbell rang, and rescue was at hand. To the tune of 'You're being disrespectful,' and 'What will the neighbours think,' I climbed unto my bike and joined my friends on a much-needed trip to the Pound.

I smiled at the faces turning as we passed. Thirty or so bikes eventually joining together to roar down the main road into the city. We always did a sort of circumnavigation of the city centre to show off I suppose or just for the hell of it. This sunny spring Saturday the town was packed, and we waved back at those who waved at us and joy filled me again.

We parked in the bus station car park, clipping our helmets to the back handrail of our bikes. It always surprised me that they were there on our return, but I suppose no one wanted to take the chance with thirty or so hairy bikers. We walked across the street, laughing and jostling, paid our entrance fee and tried to find a seat with a table in front of the stage. Pints were ordered and drunk and the talent looked over and marked. If we were lucky, and it is no reflection on me that most of the time we were, a few of those marked and noticed were invited to join us.

The PA system was playing classic rock songs from all our favourites, everything from Van Halen to Pink Floyd, and I was just mellowing and feeling alive again, but the boys were their usual raucous selves and were getting into loud bantering matches left, right and centre. This was our place. Our place for as long as we were in it. This made us the centre of attention in many respects. It wasn't that there were no other men present, but they always seemed to me to blend in with the furniture, stay on the outskirts if you will.

The group of girls who joined us that Saturday were nurses at the Royal Victoria Hospital and like us, only concerned with living for the day. A smallish girl next to me asked me if I would move up so that her friend, who was at the loo, could get a seat. I was happy to oblige, not even a frisson of desire, I was seemingly indifferent to female company that day.

I was dwelling on the helmet thing and tuned out of the conversation. In the years that I was in the bike club I never saw any member incite violence. Strange how the public perception overrides reality. Sure, some of them were big fuckers, some were huge, and some were huge fat hairy fuckers and all of them liked to drink too much. Plenty of pub nights had turned bad but not one at our behest. Mostly someone would start something, big bikers would stand up and that was it. Things calmed down immediately, and we got on with the serious matter of drinking and having fun.

This was a bike club that visited a special needs school once in a while — one of the girlfriends was a teacher there — and having roared up to the door to scare/thrill the kids we would act as taxi drivers taking all and sundry for a ride. Some would laugh as they drooled, and some would scream with the speed and the air flying into their faces but they all would ask for more. Even those a bit less able to move, were promptly lifted out of their wheelchairs, plunked on the back and strapped together with the rider for some whizzing around the ring road. They were glorious days for the kid's laughter was so genuine and infectious.

Jet black hair caught out of the corner of my eye dragged me to back to reality with a jolt of adrenaline. Karine had turned the corner from the corridor leading to the loos and I turned my head and stared at her as she walked across the room, weaving through the other tables, all cat like and smooth, to the seat beside me. 'Howdy Sherriff,' she drawled, in a fake western accent, 'come to run me out of town again.'

To quizzical glances from her friends I stuttered, 'N', N', No. I'm just out for the music and a few drinks.'

'Shame,' she said, turning slightly to her friend. 'I could do with being ridden out of the place.' Was it my imagination or was there a pause between 'ridden' and 'out'? They all giggled at this and she added, 'You know, the Sheriff here once threw me out of a church by the scruff of my neck.'

'What. What! I did not!' I protested.

'Yep. Like I was a hooker trying to bag one of the mourners. He marches over, "Sling your hook slut or you'll feel the back of my hand." I had to slink out with my tail between my legs and everyone looking at me. Très embarrassing I can tell you.'

'Jesus,' I muttered to the general laughter directed at me, 'I think I'll get a pint.'

I went up to the bar and ordered and before the drink came, I felt someone squeeze in beside me. Clouds of hair and that warm scent and laughing green eyes.

'Do you come here often?' she said with a slight laugh.

I turned slightly towards her so that I could look directly at her, 'What is your name anyway?' I replied, ignoring the question.

She leaned one slim, toned arm on the bar, 'Hmm. Are we

on a first name basis then?'

I was squashed against her by someone else pushing in behind me and didn't mind it in the slightest, 'Well, given that I'm intimate with your profession and it's my job...'

She didn't seem to mind the crush either as she made no move to get away, 'Karine,' she replied. 'Now are you going to buy me a drink or what?'

'Okay. What will you have? And by the way my name is...'

'Sheriff — now and for always. To me anyway,' and she looked at me with those green eyes. 'What sort of bike do you have?'

'A 750 Yamaha, silver and black,' I said.

She paused for few seconds to make sure we were making eye contact, 'You must take me for a ride on it someday,' again the small twist of the mouth smile as she grabbed the pint I had bought her and walked away.

I wondered why I had not noticed how tall she was before. In her bike boots she was barely an inch shorter than me, an unusual circumstance but one I found I liked.

I also found out that I was not indifferent to female company after all and spent the next hour or so, before the band came on, completely entranced. She laughed and touched me a lot and when the band started playing and we could barely hear a thing, I leaned close and shouted into her ear.

'Would you like to come to Bangor with me on my bike, I've to collect something?' and a strange thing happened to me. I had my lips to her ear and had the smell of her hair and the warm scent coming off her skin where her neck met her shoulder bathing me, and I felt complete. Something I had been missing was now found.

Many a time after, when we would lie in bed talking about

things, she would chat away, lying on her back and partially on me, I would have my face stuck to her hair and neck, my lips against her ear just to feel that way again.

We danced, bouncing up and down on the chairs as was the *mode-du-jour* in the Pound, because by this time the place was bunged, and you could barely move. No one cared about maximum occupation or fire regulations. We sang our hearts out at all the classics, and in the small pause before the final song we turned towards each other to kiss. What a thing that was, the anticipation, the closeness, her pupils dilated, her lips moistened and then I leaned in and head-butted her.

Seven people died and twenty-four were badly injured. We, mostly cushioned by the press of bodies, walked away and secretly trembled at the thought of the fire that hadn't been. The car bomb had targeted the Law Courts across the street and — thank whatever or whoever you wish — had parked slightly round the corner. Unfortunately, I had given Karine two black eyes and I thought that she would never speak to me again.

She was sitting on the curb beside an ambulance and I walked over and sat down beside her.

She shuffled a little closer to me, 'When are we doing this 'ton-up' on your bike then?' she asked me, hand holding the side of her head. My heart banged against my ribs.

'Any time you like. Do you have a phone number?' I replied.

'Nah! Let's not do that. Let's just go now.'

I was flabbergasted.

'Sure,' I said, and I took her elbow and helped her to her feet. We walked away from the mess to the bus station car park. No one moved to stop us, why would they? Everyone was covered in dust and some in blood. People sitting crying on their own or wandering around screaming, people holding on to others dead or not. Ambulance crews and Fire crews and RUC digging in the rubble seen faintly through the fog, sirens in the distance as the Felix boys arrived (the emblem of the army bomb disposal technicians).

I took us to where my bike was parked with the others and I unlocked the chain that I kept around the front wheel, put it over my head on one shoulder like a sash and locked it again. I looked at all the other bikes sitting there and back at her. She gave me a slight nod and I went and took the spare helmet from the bike box on Kitson's Kawasaki and handed it to her. I then threw my leg over the seat, and once I had both feet on the ground again, she climbed on behind me. Not a novice then, I thought.

I pulled out and weaved though some cars abandoned on the road and headed for the dual carriageway out of town. Once past the airport on the road to Holywood, I gave it some throttle and tapped her on the hip with my hand, she looked over my shoulder and I could feel her smiling at the needle on the speedometer pointing to one hundred miles an hour.

The traffic lights at the small town were coming up quickly so I slowed down. A few minutes past them she tapped me on the shoulder and pointed at the road sign to Crawsfordburn Country Park.

I turned off and wound through the narrow roads of the Country Park. The leaves were still budding from the trees and the virgin vibrant green, unsoiled by exposure to wind or wild was glorious with the sunlight shining through and about them. I slowed down and bumped over the ramps set on the road to reduce speed and, ignoring the signs telling me not to, drove up and parked on the pathway by the beach.

It wasn't really cold, but I don't think we could have cared what temperature it was. We walked for miles down the beach and let the wind blow the remaining dust and grit out of our hair. In the next small cove over we moved a little towards the sea and she took my hand. The rocks here provided a bit of shelter from the wind and just where the soft sand ended, she took off her jacket and sat on it. I did the same and joined her. We said nothing, but after a few moments she leaned into me and started crying. I held her and her crying triggered an intense shaking in me.

They say that the evolutionary response to a close escape with death is sex, some immediacy, once vividly reminded of our mortality, to ensure our line.

I think the man walking his dog was surprised.

The Sailor's Rest

It was difficult to tell if this area was Orange or Green, probably neither. Probably harking back to a much older divide between the town's folk and the foreign interlopers from across the oceans. Some remnants of the old narrow fronted premises remained, fading paint denoting Chandlers, Rope and Sail makers and Stevedore agents. Several of the buildings in the square facing the dock had been left to rot, but a few had been demolished to make way for a new restaurant with European style outdoor tables under an awning. Beside this, separated by a tight alley, was a seventeenth or eighteenth century original looking dockland bar.

It was a miserable day, mostly overcast, the streets still wet from that morning's rain and the wind in my face brought the smell of the sea flavoured with rot. I was looking across the street at the dull paint and the faded sign proclaiming this pub as the Sailor's Rest, and trying to summon up the nerve to go in.

I brought Karine's face to mind and imagined her scorn, 'Come on, Sher. You old Cod slapper! You want to know, don't you? Get on with it. You'll not know peace until you do,' took a deep breath and walked across the cobbled street and pushed through the double doors.

There are those first few moments when entering a strange pub when the locals, protective of their domain, look you over in silence and pass judgement. The door swinging open triggers that head swivel from every person there. Maybe it is built into us, that habit — a stranger to the tribe and all that.

I ploughed on, trying best to ignore the evil looks and the noise that my shoes made on the ancient, flagged floor crossing to the bar in the sudden quiet. As I pulled at a tall, much scuffed wooden stool and sat down, judgement had been made and, as I had been found harmless, normal service resumed.

I ordered a pint of lager from the sullen barman, who poured and served it without comment. After slapping it down on the cigarette scarred bar he simply held out his hand for payment. I gave him a five and he came back with the change and a sneer and set it down in the spilled beer by my glass.

It was a strange place, obviously very old. The walls were stone, not brick, and had been whitewashed many times over the years but not recently. The windows, seemingly gungy and dirty from the outside, retained enough of their original stained-glass to look somehow beautiful from the inside. The odd shaft of sunlight illuminated the maritime scenes of sailing ships of yore, and sailors adrift in tiny boats, on mountainous seas with shining angels overhead.

A large square room with the bar, extending the length of the wall, to your right as you came in through the door. In the far two corners there were private booths, delimited by dark wooden partitions with small inset stained-glass windows. On the wall opposite the entrance there were the doors to the toilets marked Jacks and Janes and another door marked Private.

The flagged floor dipped and swayed a little here and there and was covered with a smattering of wooden topped, iron-legged tables and small round stools. None of these came anywhere near the booth directly over my left shoulder. It seemed as if there was an invisible barrier in an arc some fifteen feet from that booth against which the tables washed up.

As I glanced up, I noticed the ceiling. Even though it was covered with the residue of cigarette and pipe smoke built up over many years, or maybe many hundreds of years, it was still beautiful. The original oak was now pitch black but there was no hiding the artistry that had gone into making me feel like I was looking down on the deck of a ship.

I waited and I waited not knowing what exactly I was waiting for. The few patrons, huddled around their drinks, smoking and muttering to each other, looked like the first morning customers at any bar. Desperate in the main, destitute but for their drink and fag money and not too conscious of personal hygiene.

Around twelve thirty the double doors were pushed wide open and two large men came in side by side. They looked like identical twins, Eastern European maybe, tall, broad and fat, with babyish features and tiny piggy eyes. As they turned away from me, I could see the rolls of fat or muscle above the necks of their brown leather bomber jackets at the base of their shaved heads.

They held the doors open and a man walked in. He ignored them completely and strode over to the booth behind me like some Lord of the Manor come home from the hunt. He was about my height and build, slim with black slicked back hair, in a style belonging to an earlier age, and he was wearing, somewhat incongruously, a fur coat. A pastiche of the New York pimp possibly.

He took off this coat and hung it on a hook protruding from one of the partitions. I could see that his suit was stylish, made to measure, obviously well-tailored, out of smooth, rich cloth in a very dark blue with a hint of pinstripe. He took a silver cigarette case and lighter from the inside pocket, sat down on the faded banquette that ran around the wall of the booth while the 'twins' took up positions in front of each partition like sentinels at a Greek temple.

The barman hustled over with a bottle of gin, a bottle of tonic and what looked like a large red-wine glass and a tin bucket of ice. Did not look like that sort of place, I thought. Where the fuck had he been hiding the ice! Our friend with the coat ignored him and opening his case took out and lit a cigarette.

I thought better of asking the barman for the man's name and decided to wait a bit longer. Instead, I ordered another pint and tried to look without looking at the booth behind me by half turning to face the door and leaning, nonchalantly, I hoped, on the bar.

After a few minutes, the man said something to one of the 'twins' who came over towards me but simply barked at the barman 'Mussels' and turned and walked away, back to his station.

This place was full of surprises I thought. The barman went through the door marked Private and after a few moments came back to his bar and started wiping glasses with his none-too-clean cloth. A small bell that I had not noticed rang and he left again returning with a tray on which was a large bowl of *moules marinière*, and half a wheaten bread loaf. The smell was tantalising and my stomach which had known only lager in the last twelve hours let me know it.

As the barman hunted out some cutlery and condiments from under the counter, I caught his eye and risked it, 'Is there menu I could see?' to which came the snarled answer.

'Do I look like your fucking slave. If you want something to eat, fuck off to the place next door.'

I wisely decided not to pursue the issue, and the food, and looked down into my pint until he wandered off to deliver the mussels at the other end of the room.

Around a quarter past one a young woman came in, maybe twenty bad years old, hard used, high heels and short skirt and a bolero type jacket accentuating her copious chest. The make-up was thickly applied, a long time ago, making her look tried and haggard. She clicked and clacked across the floor and I looked down to see that her high heels, long past their best, had lost the covering at the heel, exposing their metal tips. For all that, she had a bearing and held herself straight, composed as much as possible despite her obvious fear and approached the cubicle.

A large chubby hand was thrust into her chest and stopped her dead in her tracks. The hand's owner turned his head to the man at the table behind him who looked up at the girl and nodded slightly. The hand was removed like one of those pole arm barriers at car parks and the girl walked past to the edge of the table in the booth.

'But Jessie! I turned up and did the job. These fat fuckers,' she half turned and pointed at the 'twins', 'wouldn't give me my money, I'm desperate, Jessie. Please!'

I couldn't hear all of the reply only '…drunk and lazy cunt… looked like a fucking doll… no minge on it at all… out of my sight.'

She was standing over the table looking at him as if in some sort of shock, then, 'But Jessie I've been with you for years. You can't fuck me over now. Come on, Jessie. Please. Please!' she pleaded.

'I've told you. Now fuck off!' I heard clearly, as he had raised his voice.

'You're a slimy little, dickless little fucker. Think you can cheat…' she started to respond, obviously to his dislike, and he raised his head to the 'twin' on the right, who grabbed the girl by

65

her shoulder and spun her around in front of him away from the booth.

'And Rarebit give her a small slap,' I heard.

The big fat man pushed the girl away from him to arm's length and then cracked her on the side of her face with his other hand. She flew backwards and to the side crashing into an empty table and falling over it onto the floor.

I was frozen in shock. I had never before seen a man strike a woman with anything like real force. I looked around at all the other men sitting at their tables and all were staring into their drink. Not a thing was said, not a move was made, not by anyone in the place.

What do I do? Should I put the fear of getting a hiding ahead of chivalry, or even common decency. While I debated with myself the woman pulled herself painfully to her feet sobbing piteously and, holding her cheek, left the room. I hadn't even managed to get my arse off my stool. I had never been less proud of myself. And then swamped with self-disgust I swallowed my relief like every other timid fucker in the room.

Oblivious to the waves of consternation around him the man sat with his feet up on a chair and smoked another cigarette. Most certainly he, or more likely his large minders, dominated this place completely. It was like a scene from a cut-rate Mafia movie and it was hard to believe it was real.

Every so often he scribbled into a little black book that he had taken from his coat, and around twenty minutes later an old couple came in and approached the gatekeepers. Even before they had come within an arm's length, the man at the table had muttered something and they were allowed to continue unmolested. He stood and took them by the hand in turn, 'Sit Jean. Sit Paddy. Take the weight off your feet and let me get you a drink.'

It was hard to guess their ages. They'd had a hard-scrabble existence, that was for sure. And the drink, cigarettes and lack of nutrition had played their role. Maybe fifty going on a suburban seventy. Both were white haired and a little stooped.

'No. No. *Ceannasaí*. We're fine. We're fine.'

'It's just Jessie, Paddy,' he interrupted.

'OK. Jessie, thank you.'

'We just came to thank you for sorting out our boy, our little Conchuir. We thought him long lost to the cause and bound for the 'H' Blocks. Or, much worse, set-up to die in some stupid ambush with those fuckers from the SAS as a cannon fodder martyr to rally new blood. You know what a hothead he is. Not suited to the rank and file at all.'

'It was nothing, it was nothing,' he replied smugly, and just as their bums touched the seat, he grabbed at their hands again and steered them back to the outside world. They stumbled past the guards looking back and thanking him again. 'No thanks needed. Really. It was a pleasure. Just remind Conchuir he owes me a wee favour now!' he laughed as if joking. 'Go on now. Take care of yourselves. Wolfgang show them to the door,' he said to Thing Two.

The older couple left and Thing Two ambled back to his post. Things quietened down, and the man, Jessie the cut rate Mafioso, continued to smoke and write into his little book. The bartender waited for the nod and then wandered over to clear the dishes, and I had almost made my mind up to as to where Jessie's allegiance lay when his next 'customer' threw a spanner into the works.

A woman, early middle thirties, attractive and poised and beautifully groomed appeared in the doorway. Her long leather overcoat was unbuttoned to give a glimpse of a sensible blouse and skirt, tights and well-polished black leather shoes. She strolled up to the booth, with that sinuous hip movement beloved of cat-walk superstars, barely glanced at the boy boulders, walked past and sat down in the single chair facing the U-shaped banquette. She glared at our man who took his time looking up from his book. He then took his time looking her slowly up and down.

'What can I do for you today then?' he said, with a rather reptilian smile. So, it wasn't her first interaction with the scumbag. 'Would you like a cigarette, a drink?'

'No thank you. I still don't smoke,' she breathed in and poised herself. 'I've thought about what you said and I'll do what you ask,' she said almost too softly for me to hear.

'With enthusiasm and as if you're loving every minute of it?' he asked, leaning towards her eagerly.

'Yes. And you'll do as you say? You'll talk to those effers at the UVF, or whatever you call them and get them to leave my Harry alone?' Was that a hint of defeat in her voice?

'That is our agreement, once you do your bit. I'll do mine,' he replied, sitting back against the booth wall now, confident that he'd won whatever prize he'd been aiming for.

'Fine,' she said and got up, smoothed her skirt down over her hips and started to walk away. She turned after a moment, 'How do I know I can trust you?'

'You can't, but you can,' he smiled, and you could see the snake oil shine. 'Put on a show, a woman like you, and I'll help you, don't you fear.' The woman walked past the punters, threading her way through the tables, who as one, stopped drinking to eye her up again as she pushed her way out through the double doors.

It was time I thought.

I sank the remainder of my pint and dragged myself, kicking and screaming inside, to the booth at the other end of the room. I put on a smile when the hand forced me to a stop. It was like walking into a steel pole. 'Could I have word?' nodding in the direction of his boss.

The rhino holding me back looked behind him and said 'Chief?' After a few seconds examination came the slight nod, and I was allowed to approach.

'What do you want?' he said, putting his feet back up on the chair that I was about to sit down on, recently vacated but still slightly redolent of expensive perfume. A bit aggressive I thought. No introductions. No pleasantries. Obviously meant to unsettle me.

I jumped right in, 'I'd like to talk to you about what happened with my wife.' I think if I'd had less to drink, I would have thought about the absurdity of this situation. Why the fuck should he have any idea what I was talking about.

'Look son,' he interrupted me condescendingly, he was my age for Christ's sake. 'Go and take it up with her. They come for a job and I pay them — big deal — just business. If you can't handle it, then tough shit. Should have been a better husband.' And he waved his hand at me in dismissal.

'No,' I said, 'that's not what I mean. I…' as at his nod a large shovel-like hand clamped onto my shoulder and pulled me away.

He stood up now and gestured towards the door, 'I'm sick to the back teeth with boyos like you coming in here and giving me grief about the wives and girlfriends. Fucking grow a spine! Show them a little grit or better still the back of your hand and they will soon wise-up. Fucking sick of you pricks. Rarebit! Take him outside and give him a slap. But Rarebit,' he paused and looked Honey Monster one in the eye, 'a slap. OK. Wolfgang go with him and make sure it does it right.'

A similar shovel-like hand clamped onto my right shoulder and Dozer one and Dozer two simply grasped tighter and lifting me off my feet walked me to the door. I squealed with the pain and shouted for them to let me go while the other pub patrons laughed at my predicament, secure in the knowledge that while I was the centre of attention, they were safe.

I squirmed and kicked ineffectually and gasped with relief as they took me outside and let me go. For a moment in the wind and rain I thought about how lucky I was and what a close shave I'd had and how I couldn't wait to get home and shower that place from me. What the hell had I been thinking; this had been beyond stupid.

I walked a few steps towards the curb, freedom beckoning, only to be spun around again to face the 'twin' apes. They nodded to each other and then slapped me.

In retrospect I am glad that their timing was a little off, for if they had hit me simultaneously, I believe my skull would have shattered, and I have no doubt that that was their intention.

As it was, the slap from my left hit first, knocking me to my right a fraction of a second before the slap from my right landed. Fortunately, or unfortunately, I will never know, that made the strike from my right hit me more on my jaw than my cheek. The pain was excruciating, a car crash without seatbelts. My left ear drum burst, and my jaw broke, and the pain made me throw up. I was still standing, only because the force from each cancelled the other out, but slowly fell to my knees on the wet flag stones with one hand over my ear and the other holding my jaw, and then fell forward, mewling with the agony, blood coming out of my nose, ear and mouth to crack my forehead on the pavement while the pain took me away.

Sometime later I was aware of a light and the stabbing pain in my head made me sick again. I was still on my knees, soaking wet, with my forehead on the concrete and a pool of blood and vomit under me keening like a banshee.

'Fuck's sake. Would you look at this one. What a state!' a voice said. 'I'm not getting that fucking stuff on my uniform. Put a call into the Seaman's mission to see if some kind soul will come and help him to a bunk.'

The light was occluded a little. 'Sarge. I don't think he's a pisshead. Look at his clothes and his shoes. Might have been mugged. Here son, lift your head up.' A hand under my chin lifted my head and I screamed and went away again.

There were vague images of a grey steel floor bouncing and vibrating with occasional wafts of smoky diesel, and pairs of polished boots resting on me like I was a footstool, a half remembered, 'Put on the blues and twos, will yee. I want to get this dumped at the Royal and us off to the chippy before closing.' Then the Land Rover must have hit a ramp in the road a little too fast as I bounced up with the rest of them but landed hard on the floor howling.

I woke in a bed in the hospital, a side room. There were those sounds, familiar and somehow reassuring. My head was clamped in position, wires wound around my face. The pain in my jaw, ear and head had faded to a dull roar and I let the tears run down my cheeks.

A week later I had recovered enough to leave hospital, the surgery on my jaw and eardrum had been pronounced successful and I could just about manage on my own with straws and a procession of liquid meals.

I had no one to talk to anyway.

The Bedroom

It was six months to the day since my mother had euphemistically passed on. If her and her God were together then rather him than me. It would not be long until he was finding excuses to take the 'dog for a walk' or 'work on the car'.

It started to rain as we came out of the registry office, so we just ran pass the dozen or so well wishers, who had assembled outside after the ceremony to hurl the confetti and jumped into the car conveniently parked at the curb. I wound down the window and shouted at the gathered, 'Just follow us home.'

I remember little of the reception we had arranged at what was now our house because I had an almighty need to be rid of everyone and be alone with my wife. They were bleating and blahing and drinking and noshing and I made it clear in my speech that consummation would take precedence over their partying. They thought that I was kidding until we started pushing them out shortly after dessert.

I was sitting on the bed prematurely naked perhaps, slowly taking the seemingly hundreds of pins out of her hair prior to helping her off with her wedding dress. She was not helping things by occasionally, 'accidentally' brushing against me.

'I finally get to be with a married woman,' I joked, moving to the edge of the bed to get at the pins at the back of her head.

'You've forgotten your Welsh floosy,' she replied.

'Nothing actually happened, as you know,' I said, a bit deflated.

'Come here,' she said, taking my hand from her hair, standing up and turning to face me on the bed. She held both my hands now and putting them on her dress at her knees used them to help peel up her dress to her hips, 'I suppose I should be flattered that I'm now the WILF!' laughing that little seductive laugh that turned my guts inside out.

The sun sank early or maybe we just didn't notice the time passing, and through the Velux overhead we watched the most beautiful full moon start its passage across the star-encrusted black velvet sky.

'I know you don't believe in all that spiritual nonsense or mystical healing or ghostly or spooky goings on, but we are aligned in so many ways,' she said softly, while lying on top of me face up, head on my shoulder.

'How so?' I murmured, into the back of her hair.

'My mother was also a cunt!' she said, as she slipped off me to lie by my side and turn her head towards me

I waited tremulously, like a little field mouse afraid to breathe, in case the hawk comes to end its life with a razor-sharp swipe and a piercing beak. Was she actually going to…?

'Yeah, a right junky, fuck-up of an alcoholic cunt!'

Home Sweet Home

Her house was a prefab thing, constructed on a space between an electricity sub-station and a small dirty river. Her father made of it what he could, in between sparse work as a freelance local news journalist.

Her mother worked at a variety of jobs, mostly fast-food outlets and supermarkets but she took it as read that he would be home with the kids and therefore took advantage. Her favourite phrase was, 'Would you shut-up! I'm entitled to a night-out!' as she slammed the door and headed God knows where, often to be missing at breakfast.

She remembered dinner times when her father would cook something from what little he could buy, always inventing little things to make them smile; like, spelling out their names in spaghetti or cutting the bread and toasting it in the shape of their initials. Or her favourite; making shapes out of mashed potato, like ships with sausages for funnels or mountains with little bits of broccoli spread about in it like trees and always with a lake of gravy lapping at the foot of the mountain.

After dinner, when they had washed and put away, it was story time. His glorious stories of strange people and places and the adventures they had, would have her entranced, and on many nights, they would continue, as she fell asleep in the bed she shared with her little brother, filled with a wistfulness and a longing for something she could not put a name to.

These were happy times, full of laughter and wonder, but all too often the door would burst open and that smell would waft in. Wine and cigarettes, sometimes the smell of sweat, hers and others.

The first words out of her mouth were almost always abusive, 'Get you two wee fuckers to bed!' or, 'Why the fuck are they still up? Sort them, so I can have some peace.'

This was invariably followed by her throwing herself on the couch and opening the wine she had brought home. Sometimes, it was, 'Make me some dinner you lazy bastard! I need to line my stomach and get out to the pub.'

When we remember something that is laced with negative emotion, we see in our mind's eye only the troughs relating to those events, never the peaks, so it is that her memories of family life are almost unbearably bleak. As an adult, she has looked at those memories and wondered why her father put up with her mother and her behaviour, and the answer she suspects, is in the occasional times she saw her father staring after her mother with that look, a look that she has only now come to know through her own relationship. It is the same look in Sher's eyes when he comes home, as she waits, standing right inside the door to be the first thing he sees.

This could well have gone on all throughout her young life, but these things have a way of coming to a head and it was the day of the Halloween party at school and her father was trying to make something out of the bits of cloth that he had scavenged. Perhaps it was to be an angel's wings for her and a devil's headdress for her brother. The dinner table was covered in bits of paint and Sellotape and all the other paraphernalia needed for these occasions.

Her mother came home early, blouse not buttoned correctly, lipstick a little smeared and smelling strongly of cigar smoke.

Breezing in and insisting that she and her brother go and sit in front of the TV so that she could talk to 'That gobshite of a father.'

She does not remember the conversation, only that it seemed to concern money, her father's voice at first placating and soft, her mother's strident and loud. It seemed to go back and forth for ages with her mother's tone changing from desperate, to pleading, to contemptuous. She did hear the last things though. Her father shouting, shocking in itself, 'Just stop! Just take it and go out and leave us in peace.'

He slapped his hands on the table and glared at her mother, and as he got up and pushed past to go and sit with the children by the TV, her mother grabbed the scissors he had been using, and snarled, 'Don't you turn your back on me, you fuckwit waste of space!' lashed out and stabbed him in the neck.

She remembers the blood. She had run into the kitchen when she heard the loud grunt. It seemed to her eight-year-old self that she was in a shower of red water. It was pumping out of her father's neck all over her head and running down into her eyes, and as she moved closer, with her arms out to embrace him, as she opened her mouth to scream 'Daddy', he fell to his knees then slowly unto his side. He looked into her eyes and tried to say something, but then his eyes lost focus, and he just stopped moving, and breathing, and went away. How, how could this happen so fast, where did he go and how did she get him to come back. She sat at his side, crying, blood still running down her face and her nightdress while her mother grabbed at some money on the table and brushed past on her way out the door.

She next saw her mother three weeks later at school.

Her and her brother had held on to her father's body until it had gone cold. Then, not knowing what else to do, she washed them both as well as she could, brushed his little teeth for him and went to bed where they held on to each other all through that longest night.

In the morning she took her brother to the nearby school as usual, but the teacher at the gate, spotting their dishevelled state, asked her where her father was, and she had to say that he was on the floor in the kitchen and that he would not get up. The teacher didn't ask about her mother.

She remembers little of that time after, bright lights and old people in suits, and a woman pretending to be kind, and a cold bed in a long room with other children crying themselves to sleep. Her and her brother finally together in a house with a middle-aged couple. They were kind but distant and she didn't like the way the house smelled. She remembers that the doors inside the house were red and that the carpet looked like a striped animal and that they wouldn't let her and her brother sleep in the same bed or even in the same room.

Weeks went by with visits from grown-ups asking questions she couldn't answer. Mostly she remembers the cold meat and hot potatoes for dinner, which was very strange, and nights in bed curled up shivering and crying and constantly trying and failing to sneak into bed with her brother.

After those few weeks had passed, the old couple took them back to school in their little blue car and the teacher was suddenly very clingy, and huggy, and touchy, which she did not like at all. She only wanted to be with her brother and when playtime finally came, she ran over to him and dragged him to a corner of the playground under the trees away from the other kids, where they sat on a log and held each other.

That was when mother came.

She smiled at them and told them how glad she was to see them, how she'd come to rescue them and how things would be okay now. She urged them to hurry and to climb up onto the wall at the edge of the playground where she hissed at them to jump down and she would catch them. When they had done so, excited and a little frightened, she snatched up their hands and dragged them across the street and around the corner to a waiting black car.

She was trying so hard to be nice, and cool and motherly, but Karine could see that her heart wasn't in it. Asking them how they were and had they had enough to eat. She was jumpy and twitchy, and her nose was running a lot. Every few seconds, thinking they wouldn't notice, she would wipe the snot on her coat sleeve, and she had what looked like sick in her hair, and now that they were close, she smelled unwashed.

She bundled them into the back seat and pushed in after them. When she closed the door, the car took off a little too quickly, before they had time to get their seat belts on, but mother didn't seem to care. She just leaned back into the seat and closed her eyes.

The man driving the car smelled like an old bin. He kept saying, 'Right love, nearly there, you're doing the best thing.' But they weren't nearly there. Karine thought that it took another thirty minutes or so before they turned into a lane that led alongside the river and pulled into a warehouse.

Her brother had fallen asleep on her shoulder in the car and the warehouse was bright with fluorescent light. The sudden noise of the metal gate coming down woke up and frightened him, so she took him into her arms and rocked him gently. The man opened the back door of the car and ushered them out. He then led the way through a small brown door marked Private to a corridor that opened out onto a film set.

On a stage were five chairs arranged in a semi-circle around a table-come-stool like thing. In front of this on the whitewashed floor were two film cameras, one man holding headphones and a long microphone, and a soft canvas chair, in which sat a short, bald, stocky man smoking a small cigar.

Karine was hauled across the room, feet dragging on the concrete floor, and pushed into a chair set against the wall. The man dragging her hissed at her to stay put no matter what or he would slap her. He pushed her mother, who had followed aimlessly, into a chair alongside and reached into his pocket and gave her some white powder. She immediately became much more animated and livelier and rushed off to the toilets in one corner of the warehouse.

Her brother was carried over and set down in front of the bald man who looked at him for a few seconds in silence then nodded. The smelly car man jumped up unto the stage and pulled her brother up after him. He then told him to undress and when her brother shook his head, he quickly stripped him naked, holding him with one arm while his little white body shuddered with cold and fear. He tied him face down on to the table thing and Karine could see the tears running down his cheeks and hear him crying and pleading, 'Mama, Mama!' The man then reached into a jar under the table and smeared some sort of paste between his legs from the back and said 'Ready.'

A door opened at the back and five men walked in and stepped up unto the stage. They ranged from slim and late thirties to fat and soft and middle aged, and all were dressed in long, not too clean, white dressing gowns, two were wearing white hoods with eye holes that made them even more frightening.

The short bald man stood up and approached them and laid out the rules, raising his voice over the boy's cries. Each was to have a short turn — entry followed by no more than five strokes

— before the lucky guy selected first got to finish. Then it was mucky all the way down as drawn by lot earlier. He warned them though, to use no names, and above all else to keep their heads up so that he could keep their faces out of the frame. In return he would give them superb POV shots and tight close-ups of the action. Lastly, he mentioned, that since all funds had been gratefully received, each of the only five copies of the print would be hand delivered within seven days.

With that he returned to his chair and shouted 'Action!'

Her mother came back from the loo, and Karine, looked up at her with dread, 'Mummy?' Her mother glanced at her with a wild smile and white stuff stuck to her nostrils. 'Mummy, please!'

'What the fuck do you want, you little daddy's girl!' her mother sneered.

'Mummy! Help him! Help him!' Karine pleaded in desperation.

'He's fine, it'll do him good, probably enjoy it. Just you wait and see,' her mother said, drifting out and slumping back against the wall with her eyes closed and her mouth open.

From the stage a little boy screamed in terror and pain. As Karine jumped up and ran towards him, a large arm swung out and beat her to the floor. Her brother was still screaming and Karine started to crawl towards him.

'I fucking warned you, you little bitch!' growled the smelly man. He picked her up by the front of her green school jumper and holding her out at arm's length, he slapped her, slamming her into the wall, smashing her head and knocking her unconscious.

When she woke up, Karine was unable to open her left eye and there was a jack-hammer pain on that side of her head. Blood was caked in her hair and had run down to coagulate on her face and on the side of her mouth. The sound of snoring near her was like someone stabbing her in her eye. Her mother was propped up on the chair beside her.

'…and what about her.' She saw the smelly man point at her while talking to the bald man.

'I think it best if she went to the Sisters. On the way there throw that heap of shite,' the bald man was nodding towards her mother whose snoring had hit an apnoea stop, 'into the fucking river, for all I care.'

'What about the boy?' the smelly man said moving to pick her mother up with his arms under hers.

'Don't worry, I'll have Charlie sort him at the incinerator,' the bald man replied while walking off and waving. 'Cheerio now.'

She sat half turned in her seat, her aching face pressed against the lovely cool, soothing wall and listened to the sounds of the man struggle to force her comatose mother into the black car. Then the footsteps as he came back towards her.

She felt the smelly man grab her arm and pull her to her feet. She tried to walk but she was dizzy and wobbly and fell and banged her knees painfully on the concrete floor. Cursing at her, he grabbed her by the scruff of her jumper again and carried her dangling in one hand past the stage to the door and the car.

It was difficult to see, but she caught a glimpse of a small, unmoving pale white body with far too much blood around its thighs, legs and feet. She immediately started to squirm with all her might and shouted for help at the top of her voice. The man just held her out from his body so that she couldn't kick him and walked on, throwing her into the boot of the car, slamming it shut and driving away.

Karine curled up in a ball around her pain, and cried,

heartsick and sore, for her lost brother and for the comfort of her father's arms.

I had absolutely no idea what to say and was terrified of saying the wrong thing anyway, so I slid my arm under her and pulled her to me. She resisted for a few seconds and then sagged against me tucking her head into my neck. She stared to sob — in all the time I had known her I had only once before heard her cry, and that was at a fraught and desperate event in our lives — and she sounded so much like a little girl locked in the boot of a car that I found my tears running in sympathy.

After some time, she lifted her face, all teary and blotchy and said, 'I think I win,' and got up and went to the loo.

She made a detour to the kitchen on the way back and surprised me with Champagne, black grapes, soft white cheese and Jacob's crackers. 'Who knew,' she smiled. 'Confession makes you hungry. Get your eyes off my goods and unto the goodies.' The smile was a little forced but I smiled along with her, in an effort to help.

We settled down to a messy snack and cared nothing for the bed sheets. Champagne from belly buttons is only nice if it is from the female receptacle, I discovered. Soft cheese makes a pleasant body lick and cracker crumbs do get into every crack — I was astonished to discover a little later.

With the mood changed, now relaxed, warm and cuddly, I risked continuing things.

'Your mother?' I asked tentatively.

'Who the fuck knows. I certainly don't, and I couldn't give a flying-fish pig shit. I most fervently hope that the raddled bitch died with her hole eaten by syphilis in a ditch somewhere ice cold, after having acid thrown in her face. I hope she drowned slowly as the ditch filled with rain, blubbing but unable to scream properly as her eyes went blind and the acid tore her throat to pieces.' She took a deep breath, and I could she see was forcing herself calm again.

'I've decided, that because you were exceptionally good at conquering the soft cheese nipple challenge, but really because I sort of like you, to tell you everything — shit and Shinola — as the old folks used to say,' she said, pulling her legs under her and sitting in that way that females can but males find so uncomfortable.

There was a definite lightening of the sky by this time and although I was exhausted, it was a happy exhaustion and I certainly did not want to stop her now.

'Shit and Shinola! You don't look like you're eighty and I've examined you all over quite recently, sometimes with interesting results.' I raised myself up a little so she could squirm back and lean against my shoulder.

The St. Glaphyra Sisters of Chastity Home

Karine was a driven little girl. She escaped every day for the first nine days after she was forced into the sisters' care. At first, she was heart-sick, worried about her brother, stumbling and easy prey, but as she healed, she became more difficult to catch. Unfortunately, the grounds were very large and still surrounded by the tithed farmsteads on which many of the nun's families lived and these people were well versed in the capture and return of escapees.

On her ninth attempt she made it onto the bus on the road beyond the nearest farm to the west, but the driver would not let her travel with no money, and their heated discussion attracted the attention of the convent gatekeeper who had been on his way into town to his monthly homing pigeon society meeting.

The sprawling buildings of the convent, chapel and children's home were nearly 200 years old and had been gifted to the church by the Baron, Sir Williem Glanville De Courcy Mills. Sir Williem, euphemistically called one of the last adventurer knights, served in the Peninsular wars and had the great good fortune of falling, with his brigade, on the baggage train of Joseph Bonaparte, Napoleon's brother and King of Spain, as he fled from the advancing armies of the allies under Sir Arthur Wellesley, soon to be the Duke of Wellington.

Recorded history of the event fails to remember that he was only in position to do so due his incompetence and arrogance. His orders from Wellesley ignored or misinterpreted and advice from his junior officers disregarded, he rushed his brigade far to the left of any possibility of fighting and sweeping up a rise, discovered the baggage wagons and their pitiful defenders huddled in its slope. His duty to reinforce the 60th Regiment of Foot forgotten and overcome by greed he ordered his brigade to charge.

Many of his compatriots would have called Sir Williem a ruthless prize seeking coward, cold hearted thug and thief, but none of them choose to do so publicly. There were great riches seized that day but barely half of it made it back to King George's exchequer.

As was the custom, suspicions notwithstanding, the government awarded Sir Williem his prize share of five pieces in every hundred of the market value of the gold, gems, silks and paintings taken. Little was made of the slaughter of the hundreds of camp followers — mostly woman and children — who had travelled with the train.

Perhaps it was guilt, or the inescapable feeling of mortality catching up with him, that made the Baron, in his old age, grant the lands and the monies to build beautiful gothic buildings to a travelling Benedictine Sister of Mercy, on the grounds that she start a new order to care for homeless and orphaned children.

The St. Glaphyra Sisters as they came to be, after a martyr known for her chastity, had no intention of taking in boy children, who they perceived to be the very embodiment of the devil, and even the wasted and bedraggled girls who fell to them, needed to have their sinful souls purged with work and the lash.

This enlightened attitude was passed down the years and remains a mainstay principle of the orphanage to this day, personified by their motto which is found carved into every plinth, pillar, pedestal and pediment; *'labor omnia vincit'* — hard work conquers all.

Karine was put in the 'contemplation and regard for sinful penitent box' a six-foot square oubliette with no windows, a running stream across the floor and minimal rations. As it was her ninth time, the sisters thought that nine days and nights would be appropriate. She was still only eight years old.

It broke her.

Years passed and at around puberty the girls started to receive lessons in how to be a good Catholic Christian woman from the incumbent priest. This, because it was out of the ordinary, was the most exciting thing and was endlessly discussed and analysed and dreamed about. However, it didn't take long until the monotone lecturing from the middle-aged man about their need to be obedient to their husbands at all times and in all things, about their need to acquire and practice wifey skills, like cleaning, sewing and cooking began to pale, and the girls started to dread the weekly drudgery.

A strange thing happened to change the communal feeling for this lesson. At the end of the first month a girl called Sonia was singled out for praise and was awarded a private, reverent meeting one-on-one with the Father in his rooms after Vespers.

This selection, this prize, was now talked about constantly and speculated upon by those who had not been chosen. The fact that the chosen said nothing and nothing could draw comment from them, simply made the mystery more enticing.

In a world where downcast, beaten, and broken girls was the norm. Where to look a sister in the eye meant immediate censure, where disobedience or failure to jump to a command meant a day in the 'contemplation and regard for sinful penitent box', a change in the demeanour of any particular girl, unless it was towards happiness, would go unremarked upon, unnoticed and irrelevant.

All Karine noticed was that she hadn't been chosen. She continued to notice when she wasn't chosen the next month or the month after that. This began to grate on her, hadn't she been an ideal student, pious and devout in her prayers and catechism? Because of this a little of her previous character awoke and she decided that, despite the risks, she would ask the sisters why.

Churning this over, waiting for her chance, her mind restless day and night, the unfairness, the injustice that was being perpetrated eased her awake further, and as a result, especially in those just before sleep moments, she remembered the outside and her earlier will to escape.

That month's 'prize' eluded her again. After the priest had left, she lingered until all the other girls had passed her by on their way out of the classroom and she coughed slightly to attract the attention of the sister on chaperone duty.

'Sister?' she enquired timidly.

Sister Mary-Louise Altagracia Kelly looked up from her desk, she was a little taken aback but was still in a nice warm, rosy sort of mood after having caned two girls caught whispering to each other earlier that morning. 'What can I do for you, my child?' she said, closing her Bible.

'Sis. Sis. Sister.' Karine stuttered a little, 'I'm trying so hard, but can't seem to win the monthly prize with the Father. Is there anything else I can do?'

Sister Mary-Louise stared at her for a few moments and Karine immediately looked down at the floor, she got up and walked around her desk to stand over Karine, 'Have you prayed child?'

'Yes sister. I pray long and hard to be chosen.'

Karine could feel her gaze, it seemed to burn into the top of her head like a search light and for a moment it appeared that the sister was muttering to herself in prayer, 'Well, perhaps then God will answer you.'

Perhaps God indeed answered her, for he/she/it is known for their malicious sense of humour and the next month, at the end of the lesson, Sister Brigid Celestina McGann announced to the class that Karine was that month's prize winner.

Karine trembled with a little fear but mainly anticipation when two sisters came for her after Vespers and took her to a small bathroom near the Mother Superior's rooms. Here they made her strip completely, shift, socks and underwear. They washed her body and her hair with that none-to-gentle approach that seemed to exemplify their attitude to every task that necessitated touching a girl.

After dressing her in a long white nightgown, they took her to a part of the Chapter House she'd never seen before. They walked along a beautiful parquet floored corridor, framed on one side by intermittent stained-glass windows depicting scenes of saints' martyrdom that had not yet reached her in her religious education. On the other side, the plain white wall was hung with portraits of various Popes going back into antiquity.

At the end of the corridor was a vestibule, lit during the day by sky lights in the high ceiling above, but now by a massive chandelier with dozens of small bulbs replacing the once original candles, and covered with a thick woollen carpet which was a deep dark shade of red.

Karine was awed by the absence of sound as she and her guardian sisters stepped on to it from the wooden floor. They walked straight ahead to a large solid, plain brown door, hung into a pale sandstone arch shaped frame and bearing a gold plaque on which was described the legend 'Father Confessor

Perpetual'.

One of the sisters knocked quietly and opened the door while the other pushed Karine gently inside. The door was immediately closed behind her and not the slightest sound of the sisters walking away could be heard.

After a few moments Karine lifted her head and looked around. On her left was a fireplace in front of which was a faded red and gold Persian rug bookended by old brown leather chairs, the sort with high wing like protuberances at neck and head height to cut down on draughts.

To her right the wall was completely obscured by floor to ceiling bookshelves, packed to the edges and overflowing so that some books were stored horizontally on top of the racks of vertical ones. Straight ahead was a large window and to each side of that, in the corners of the room opposite her and the door, stood tall standard lamps with conical beige lampshades, fringes dangling. In front of the window was a huge oak desk with a red leather panel inset and on which was absolutely nothing at all. Behind it, in a more modern but still aged leather chair, was the priest.

The room smelled of mould and a certain muskiness, whiskey and old cigarette smoke, and it was perhaps this smell above all else that fully restored Karine to herself. It was as if she had been behind the scenes watching her own life and had now stepped forward to take up the reins once more. She was still coming to terms with this wonder when she heard him say, 'I said, come and stand over here my dear and let me look upon you.'

Karine moved to the side of the desk and could see that the man was sitting in his black shirt with his dog collar but below that in just his underwear, old looking, faded white, baggy things, that allowed his fat hairy thighs and incongruously thin lower legs to show. She noticed a ring of baldness a few inches up from his ankles and was concentrating on this trying to understand, 'Please don't be offended by my dress. I have a condition and must let the air to my lower body as much as possible,' he said as he turned his chair to face Karine directly.

'Socks,' she said, pleased with herself, 'that's where the elastic on your socks tightens.'

The priest looked at her rather askew, thrown a little, 'Come closer child,' paused for a moment to recover and then said, 'Shall we pray?' Karine nervously moved to his side of the desk.

After a very long-drawn-out supplication to the Lord on all sorts of trivial matters about which Karine could not give a damn, he reached out and grabbed her hands-in-prayer enfolding them with his large hairy hands and said, 'Amen!' Then pulling her towards him, 'I must test you now child.'

He looked at the ceiling for a few seconds, as if communing with Him above, and then lowered his gaze and looking into her eyes asked with a fierce, devout tone, 'Are you a Godly child who honours our mother church and all her saints, her Holy Father, her cardinals, bishops and priests, her sisters and all the lay people who serve her?'

Karine new better than to hesitate, 'Of course, Father.'

'Do you honour her fully, with mind and body, willing to sacrifice yourself to her greater glory?' He had closed his eyes and his voice took on the fervent tone she'd often heard in mass.

'Of course, Father. With all my heart.'

'And do you accept that I am the embodiment of the church and to do my will is to do hers?

Karine didn't know what embodiment was but knew what the answer had to be, 'Yes, Father.'

'Well done my child. You've passed!' he said with huge enthusiasm, letting go of her hands. 'Now I shall need to touch you to signify my acceptance of you into this higher level of service. You need feel no shame in this, for this is God's will, but you must keep it private between us and the Lord or else fear for your immortal soul. Is that clear?' Karine nodded, her mouth too dry to speak.

'You are a good Christian, God fearing child,' and with that the holy father lent forward and pulled her nighty up over her head. Karine was shocked but the only possible response to any adult in her world was immediate silent obedience or compliance. The priest stood up and dropped his ugly underwear to the floor, 'Bend over the desk my dear.'

Karine couldn't move. Her brain was telling her to do what he said, or she would be sorry, but the bit of her that had recently awoken was telling her to leave. She was staring at the man's groin and could see nestled in the mass of grey and black hair, under his pendulous belly, something that was very much like the sausages they served for breakfast on saints' days, except this sausage looked raw and like someone had dyed the end of it with faint purple paint. It was this image, of someone painting the end of their willy purple that broke the dam and she started to laugh.

The priest was furious and grabbed her with both hands around her neck and started to squeeze. 'You little bitch! You devil's whore! Laugh at me will you! By God you will regret that. I shall crush your worthless life from you!' He picked her up and she was kicking and writhing in his grasp, her face growing redder, her little hands coming up to swat at his as she struggled to breathe. He brought her head up level with his own. The smell was appalling. Along with the cigarette smoke was sour whiskey and his awful, rotten meat, dental health ignored, odour. The last thing she thought before darkness fell was that she'd at least managed to pee down his legs and over his feet.

Karine woke on the floor, between the chairs on the red and gold mat, the pain in her neck and throat was terrifying, she felt unable to get enough air and started to gasp uncontrollably. The priest was sitting in his chair drinking whiskey from a large tumbler, he'd yet to put his pants back on. 'Death is too good for you, you harlot, you scum, you maggoty ill-begotten little child!' He was practically spitting with fury, as he was saying this, standing up to lean one hand on the desk while pointing at her with the glass.

He paused as if in thought for a few moments then set the drink down and came to stand over her, reaching down to pick her up by her throat with both hands once more. 'I'm going to squeeze you to within an inch of your life over and over again,' he was panting and salivating and this time before everything went dark, Karine saw that his sausage was sticking up in the air erect, and quivering.

When she next awoke, in the same place, she wanted to die. The priest sitting once more behind his desk, said, as if reading her thoughts, 'Go on, choose. Kill yourself, it's one way out. Otherwise, you will be here every month and every month I shall strangle you until you beg me to stuff my cock into your dry, miserable little cunt. And when you do, I might, or I might just strangle you again. Kill yourself and do us all a favour. Kill yourself and send your immortal soul back to the devil where it belongs.' With that, he grabbed her nighty off the desk and her by her hair and threw her out into the corridor shouting, 'Sisters! Take this devil's spawn away.'

The next few days were agony for Karine, she lay in bed and gasped and choked and coughed and willed herself to die. The thought of finding herself in that man's grasp too much to bear. But she didn't die. The sisters were completely unsympathetic, cursed her silently for her imagined transgressions with the Father, and ignored her as a consequence.

She slowly healed and as she did, she was able to focus more on the memory of that evening, not the pain and the terror but something else she saw as she was escorted towards the brown door.

She had managed to eat at last, some mashed potato and vegetables, and was recovering from the exquisite pain of swallowing when she saw it. In her mind's eye she saw it, a pale green sign on a faded pale grey door just to the left of the brown door, in a small alcove. 'Exit' it said.

The sisters left her alone a lot of the time thinking her, not entirely wrongly, incapable of mischief in her sickbed. She waited until the following day, Sunday, noon mass, when everyone would be in chapel, and put her hands on the floor and dragged herself out of bed and across the floor to the wall. Using this she pulled herself to her feet and hesitatingly took her first steps in days. She stumbled but got better and faster quickly. Along the stone floored corridors and two flights down, to the end on the right and the floor changed to that beautiful wood again. There at the end of this corridor was the vestibule and the brown door. She practically broke into a run until suddenly she stopped, frozen and shaking. What if he were there, she could hear his voice and feel his hands, 'Kill yourself! Kill yourself! Kill yourself!'

She might have been standing there, petrified, for hours until the sound of voices and footsteps from around the corner cracked the spell and she rushed to the alcove by the brown door to find all as was remembered. The faint green lit sign promising exit.

She pushed on the bar and the sunlight and fresh air hit her like a drug. Suddenly full of energy she quietly closed it behind her and ran for the hedges behind the chapel.

I breathed out slowly and held her tight and didn't ask her how she got away this time. I was too appalled and heartbroken for her again. How was it that my kind loving wife had emerged from this? I was too frightened to ask.

She breathed in deeply and sighed and turned her head to my neck again and kissed me. She then raised herself up unto her elbows and looked at me with those wondrous eyes and said, 'Just another un-fiddled with kiddy eh!' and then, 'Kids, so much trouble. Who the fuck would have them?'

'Yeah,' I replied, in solidarity, 'Who'd have them. Certainly not me.'

'I'm pregnant,' she said.

The Sailor's Rest

My face felt strange without its load of metal. My jaw and head ached like fuck, especially in the mornings. I assumed that the blows to my head had caused the temporarily insane state of mind I found myself in three weeks later, leading me to be standing across the road from The Sailor's Rest, hunched over in a doorway, in the freezing cold. I wasn't sure if my shivering had to do with that, or the fear I felt just looking at the place. The flesh remembers.

I had been there for an hour or so. A grey dismal day quickly becoming night, the cobbles wet with a light dusting of snow, pushed to the sides of the road by the slushing past of an occasional car or van. I watched the pub door, clocking each and every punter as they stepped into the cold, gathering their coats and scarfs about them.

Why was I putting myself through this? I should be home, lying in bed nursing my pain with self-pity and whiskey and talking to the walls. What was I waiting for?

It came in the form of Beef and Beefier and their charge, they doing their best impression of that Presidential Secret Service thing, of scanning the street while a big black car pulled up, then sheltering him under their bulk and hustling him into the back seat. I felt such relief at them driving away that I nearly wet myself a little. Not exactly what I had imagined, however.

It is a such wonderful feeling. That moment when the much-dreaded confrontation is cancelled, nullified by happy circumstance. Mine, I had to remind myself, was only postponed, better to do what must be done than suffer for fear of it — as a wise man once told me, so wise I couldn't remember his name.

I walked across the street, soft leather shoes letting in some freezing cold slush and took off my Burberry jacket to hang in front of my crotch just in case. I pushed open the door and made my way across the room, cutting through the momentary silence with the wet slapping noise of my loafers against the flagged floor and I wondered idlily if any there recognised the pale check trademark lining. Jesus wept!

The normal hubbub had resumed before I pulled out the same stool as once, I sat on, and mumbled, 'A pint of lager please' to the same surly barkeep. He set the beer down with his usual subtlety and batted not a single eyelid as I took out a straw to drink it with. I settled down to wait again.

I looked round, freely this time, and admired the windows and the woodworking again. The few drinkers that were hunched over their pints of lager or Guinness talking softly to each other were not going to keep me distracted enough to avoid the questions in my head.

Thankfully, some previous pub denizen had left a copy of the Sun newspaper on the bar and despite my misgivings — being sure that even one glance at such a rag would turn me into a right-wing slavering, national-front supporting, Nazi-tattooed, immigrant-hating nutcase — nothing happened. Pages were devoted to the upcoming visit of your friend and mine, once cardinal now Pope, Jarlath Eoghan Diarmuid O'Bannon or now to be known as Pope Francis Benedict the first. Not content with one Papal name it seems, or perhaps disinclined to be known as Pope Anyone the second or God forbid, Anyone the sixteenth. No, our man will carve out a unique course during his tenure and that will require a unique moniker. It didn't say that, of course, it's the Sun. I was reading between the lines.

Every other page had some slightly salacious story involving a celebrity or wife/girlfriend of a celebrity and their happy slappy, somewhat sexy antics and that, together with the hyped-up near hysteria of our prodigal son's return, kept me entertained for a while and kept the dread at bay.

Every good thing comes to an end and at the back end of nine o'clock the door was pushed open and the caravan of pig-shithead-pig walked in. Shithead took his place at his table, hanging up his stupid coat and pointing at Piglet One and then at the bar. He took out a comb and combed his hair, patting it into place as he finished. He then sat down and took out his cigarettes and plonked his feet up on a chair.

'He wants some o'that Champagne muck and some oysters,' the fat boar said to the barman.

'Jesus. It never gets any easier, does it?' came the much put-upon sigh, as the barman headed to the door marked Private.

'And bring him that dagger thing. You know how he likes to show off,' he rumbled, with a lilt I couldn't quite place and then waddled off back to his post, pushing through the tables and laughing at the drinks he spilled and the lack of any challenge.

About ten minutes later the door opened again and in with the cold night air came the well-to-do, elegant woman I'd seen here before. And as before, she walked past the twins like they were not there. Oh! for an ounce of her natural authority and entitlement — generations of money can do that to a girl. She sat down opposite our boy who was grinning and happy as a clam. Just then his champers and oysters arrived, delivered by the surly barman who quickly scampered out of reach and notice.

He did the usual, scanning her up and down for a minute

then, 'A little celebration is in order I think,' he said, smiling his cobra smile. 'Here watch this, I was taught by the Master of Sabrage himself.' He peeled the foil off the bottle of Veuve Clicquot — Jesus, perhaps he wasn't all that bad — untwisted the wire and removed the little metal cap from the top of the cork. He then unsheathed what looked like a World War one bayonet and holding the bottle away from him, slid the blade down the length of the bottle and through the rim. The cork exploded out, banged off the wall and landed in some greyed, wrinkled old-timer's Guinness.

'Bullseye!' he laughed and poured the bubbly into the two flutes on the table. He sat the bottle down and picked up the glasses, handing one to the woman. 'To a very successful venture, a very classy venture. Drink up and try some of these oysters, fresh off the boat.'

'You agree that our business is concluded. That I have kept my word. And furthermore, you can confirm that your intercession was successful?' she asked, sitting demurely where his feet had been, her legs crossed at the ankles and her hands on her knees.

'Yes, of course,' he replied, 'all done and dusted and your little boy safe from the slavering hounds. I am, after all, somewhat to my surprise it must be said, a man of my word.' He sat forward a little and reached out his hands towards hers, 'Now let's talk about you and another role I think you'd be absolutely the right fit for.'

She set the glass of champagne on the table and pushed back from him, then stood without replying and smoothed her skirt down over her hips. She smiled and with the glass in her hand again said, 'If you were the last man on earth, I'd kill myself before I'd drink with you, never mind do your bidding again.'

And threw the champagne over him.

As he spluttered, trying to laugh it off in front of his men, she glided past them with a such a look of contempt, daring them to touch her, that I wanted to applaud. I could swear I heard every man in the place cheering along with me — silently of course — we weren't women of class and sophistication.

Things quietened down after she had gone, and he had dried himself off and berated his porcine crew enough to make himself feel better. Then, as the number of drinkers slowly diminished, wending their way home with their carry-outs of that old stalwart — but dirt cheap — Buckfast fortified wine, I faced my demons.

'What the fuck am I doing here?' I said to Karine within. 'I must be completely looped. These fuckers will hurt me again.'

'You know why you're really here,' she replied softly. 'But we're not ready to face that yet. Roll the dice Sher.'

I looked at my reflection in the scratched and somewhat grimy mirror behind the bar and swallowed the last of my drink, 'That grim fucker from the RUC — Chief Inspector McCracken — throwing me a titbit like I'm sort of stupid toe-rag, bait for this cunt over in the corner. Did he really think I wouldn't understand what he was trying to do?'

'Succeeded though,' came the gentle reply.

'What! No, it hasn't. What the fuck has happened other than me getting smashed up around the jaw and wetting myself about confronting that greasy wanker.'

'Still going to do it though, aren't you?' she suggested.

'Yes, I'm going to do it. There must be some connection that that cop turd knows about. Something that ties you to him and that I can shake loose. That was the point in the erstwhile Kojak telling me, wasn't it?' and I rolled the dice.

Sixes! As I forced down the dread and fear and started to

ease myself off my stool, I saw the blobby twins heading for the door — presumably to do the old Secret Service thing — leaving our man alone. He was preparing to head out, grabbing his cigarettes while standing up to reach for his coat. I walked over as fast as I could weaving through the now empty tables which caught his eye. I could feel him staring at me with disbelief as I approached.

'Look son. Fuck away off and come back tomorrow, I've business to attend to elsewhere,' he said with a sneer while putting his other arm into his coat.

'This won't take a minute I promise. I just want to ask you about my wife,' I said as I came up to the table.

'Oh Fuck! I remember you. You were in here whining about your wife a few weeks ago. I thought I'd made my position cl…'

'It's not like you think,' I interrupted him. 'She wasn't working for you or anything.' And this produced for the most dreadful moment, the guilty thought that maybe she was.

'Watch it! Mackerel-dick. I only performed for you,' came the internal voice and I shook it off.

'My wife. I think you knew her in some way, her name was…' just then two massive hands with fat sausage fingers gripped my shoulders. The Secret Service had returned.

'Son. I couldn't give a slippery shit from a syphilitic monkey what her name was. You've disturbed me again, and worse, shown huge disrespect. A man like me can't have people disrespecting him, can he?' and with that he took his coat off again and hung it up.

He turned back to me with a nasty grin on his face and said, 'If I hear another word from you that is not a direct answer to a question, Rarebit and Wolfgang here are going to slap you again. Only this time it won't be gentle.' He nodded to his beefs and they picked me up as they had once before by simply gripping hard on my shoulders and lifting. He came past and led the way to the door by the bar glaring at the barman, 'Shut things up now Paddy, I need a little privacy,' and this time I think I did wet myself a little.

'People are deluded son,' him continually calling me son was beginning to irritate me, as we were much the age, but that was the least of my problems for now. I had been taken to a small room off a dank corridor with an old, much scratched and beat-about table, a few wooden chairs and a hard-wood sideboard that had once been painted green. The walls were bare plywood with various scars and dozens of staples that once, no doubt, held posters and papers extolling the members to pay their dues and such fuck. The ceiling tiles were stained with old water leaks and sagged in the corners. This was certainly a more modern extension to the original building but constructed on the cheap some years ago and ageing quickly.

I wasn't tied to the chair, but my wrists were held down tightly with my palms up, much too tightly because my hands were tingling, by leather straps that had been fed through holes in the table. I didn't want to think about that too much, about who and why someone has a table with bespoke holes for leather straps in it.

'Yes, all you poor fuckers are deluded,' he nodded at Hippo One. 'It's an old, old story. You think you live in a nice secure society with laws and morals and such. The media feed you on a diet of the good triumphing over the bad. The criminals get caught and locked away or meet their due, their grisly demise in some sort of vengefully satisfactory way. You all leave the cinema or pop on up to bed afterwards glowing, secure and happy.' Hippo One set a metal toolbox on the table and went to lean against the wall, folded his arms and glared at me.

'Now. A smart boy like you knows that the establishment, the snot-nosed aristos et al, always have the wherewithal to get themselves and their oft rebellious off-cuts out of trouble. The old boy network and all that.' He rummaged in the toolbox and took out of it, somewhat noisily I thought, a small ball-pein hammer and a narrow steel masonry chisel. He set these on the table and lifted the toolkit up for Hippo Two to take away.

'What you don't know or don't choose to accept, or simply ignore, is that all the people who have power over you are just that, people. Just the same. Just farty, shitty, belchy twats like the rest. And that means that they have the same needs and desires. They want to drink and smoke and dance and fuck, and some of them want to go further, do other nasty, slimy things that would turn your mister-normal hair white.' He picked up the hammer and chisel and holding them in the air tapped the chisel as if testing it. Clink! Clink! Clink! 'They certainly shouldn't command your automatic ingrained respect.' Clink!

'When you help them do what they want, they give themselves to you, they throw themselves into your arms, meat and spuds or udders and gash, if you prefer. They do so without hesitation and without admitting it to themselves, believing that because you provide a service you are a servant, and they do so for life.' He drew the last syllable out a little like some huckster in a fair ground as he placed the chisel in the middle of the last bone at the tip of my left-hand little finger and tapped the chisel. Clink! There was a brief flare of pain as the bone broke and a thin red line appeared on my skin leaking a little blood.

'What does this mean for you I hear you ask?' he said examining my hand. He then placed the chisel on the middle of the last bone in my ring finger, forcing it open from the clenched position I'd curled it into and Clink! Broke that bone too. He continued this way and broke all five of the Distal Phalanges on my left hand and, as my little finger began to swell at the tip, becoming red and inflamed, the pain started to hit me.

'Listen mate!' I said, gritting my teeth and starting to panic a little. 'Whatever you want you can have, whatever money I have is yours, just let's stop this foolishness and let me go,' and I tried to stand up and pull away. Immediately the thump on my shoulder from Meat One slammed me back into my seat.

'I said not to speak. Did I not!' he shouted into my face. 'I'll tell you what it means for you. You, like the rest of the masses are powerless!' he spat the 'less' at me. 'You can do nothing to the likes of me. We are protected! Free to do what we wish, to whom we wish, however and whenever we wish. And I choose to do this!' Clink!

'You went to the cops. Spilling your guts about getting slapped around by the boys here. You expected justice. You expected jail time for my pretty lads and even dared to dream of it for me, hands on the bars of my cage, regretful and guilty, staring down the barrel of a long sentence. Hmmm?' Clink!

'Oh! for sure, the local CID popped in for a chat and a free drink, they often do — bastards — and do you know what?' Clink! 'I told them everything. Just as it happened.' Clink! 'We all had a good laugh at the thought of you on your knees on the pavement outside, sick, tears, blood and rain running down your face. And then they left, still chuckling, with a bottle of my good whiskey to keep them warm.' Clink!

There are twenty-seven bones in the hand and the wrist. Distal, Middle and Proximal Phalanges. Then the Metacarpals and the mess of small bones, the Hamate and the Capitate, the Trapezoid, the Trapezium and the rest. He broke every one of them.

The pain started small enough but very quickly I was screaming, dreading the touch of that cold steel on my hand. By the time he was finished I was mewling and moaning, slobbering, drooling and begging, with my head on the table and the nightmare of my swollen and bleeding hand still tied to the table. And all the time he was doing this he talked. I wish I had the chutzpah to say something pithy like, 'Will you shut-up, your constant rabbiting is hurting me more than your chisel.' But I didn't. The flesh remembers.

Jessie

Judge Francis McDermott, the most senior judge in Ulster and permanent member of the Diplock courts — our answer to jury intimidation was trial by judge — was about his normal last Thursday in the month business. Well shaved, suited and booted he was driven to his monthly appointment, insisting that he was delivered on time no matter the traffic situation.

His close protection detail shivered outside, banned by his honour to their Ford Granada, engine off to not give themselves away and completely unable to leave the car for a smoke in case the crusty old bencher came back unannounced.

The RUC sergeant in charge, craving making him desperate, was contemplating the unthinkable and lighting up in the tank — their word for the up-armoured vehicle they trailed their charge around in. However, reason asserted itself as he remembered the aged beak's savage reaction to cigarette smoke in the car. The last time they'd let some poor newbie have a puff as a wind up, the Judge took one sniff of the tainted air and launched into the most blistering ass ripping the greenhorn had ever heard and, despite the risk, insisted that the shamefaced culprit get out and walk back to the station and never darken his door again.

The sergeant had nearly lost a stripe for that but the image of that poor bastard constable running through the streets to the safety of Ann Street Station in the rain still made him smile. You've got to take your laughs where you can in this job.

Of course, his honour wasn't allowed a say in who protected

him, so the constable turned up at some point, a few weeks later, back in the team, nervous and on the edge of panic, to find the Judge completely indifferent. The people who protected him with their lives were completely beneath him, not worthy of even having their names or faces remembered.

Lady Maude Margaret McDermott took her rose-scented, overly flowery dresses and her overly large self to her bridge club on the last Thursday of the month to indulge in a little flirting with the club captain during a mixed rubber or two. The captain, a slightly older gentleman, with a full head of white hair and an all-year round tan, had a reputation as a lady's man. Indeed, she also often flirted a little with the club captain's wife, who seemed oblivious to, or at least uncaring of her husband's peccadilloes. She treated herself in the confines of her bed, to a scandalous desire held close to her heart of enjoying them both at the same time with some good sherry and a quiche Lorraine.

On these nights of 'freedom' the good jurist would turn up at Madame du Barry's house of ill repute in Custom House Square for some light S & M — heavy on the M — and some bondage games with his regular Dominatrix — Mrs Nine Fine Chat-Tail.

Madame du Barry's, from the front an aging pub, all mosaic tiles and gilt edges but once up the stairs to the side of the public saloon bar a very different establishment. Here a quiet snug with well-worn and comfortable leather armchairs, discrete decor and dim lighting. Meals *a-la-carte* provided from a well-stocked kitchen and cooked by a chef who was trained in France. A cellar unmatched probably in the whole of the city and all served by the young and pretty, tantalisingly dressed and more importantly, available for one-on-one service at the asking, and of course the paying.

Our administrator of sentencing was well aware of the cliché — English public-school pupil rises in the establishment and indulges in behaviour seen to be, by most, beyond the pale. What can you do? He often thought. They get you young — sent by indifferent parents to board at ten years of age — dump you in with a load of sneering upper class analists and make you a fag to the worst of them. After a few years of such treatment, it seems perfectly normal, once puberty raises its heavily charged head, to inflict the same on the next tranche of inmates.

In truth, he thanked a God he fervently believed in that his parents made him come home to Northern Ireland to find his way. He could imagine nothing worse than attending a cabinet meeting in Downing Street, for instance, where many at the table had had their dick in him and he in them. How does one assert dominance in that scenario? He thought. Where the normal lines of power, when attendees may have beaten the Prime Minister with a cane while he performed fallatio on Hilde-Smythe of the lower third?

He was relaxing in the warm glow of a punishment well deserved and administered, by having his usual glass of brandy and cigar, when a young lad came into the room to clear away the wine glasses, plates and other detritus.

'Mary, who is this little guttersnipe?' he asked, in his usual too loud, dominating voice from the armchair in the corner of the room.

She was standing at the small sink wiping between her legs with a flannel, 'Madam took him in a few years back in lieu of a debt, don't think he's gonna stay much longer though 'cos he's a stinking little thief,' so saying, she reached out and grabbed the boy by the ear, 'Ain't ya. Ya wee fucking gobshite.'

'Hold yourself woman! And unhand that child!' the Judge roared. 'Come here boy and let me look at you.' Tasty young thing, the Judge thought and then shook himself, he'd left messing around with that sort of jailbait behind long ago. As the boy shyly walked towards him, head down and frightened, the Judge's idea fully took hold of him, but how to sell it?

It is amazing how little a life is worth sometimes. A young boy traded for a debt, sold onwards for a few pounds to placate a childless bitter woman who had given up on her marriage and dreamed of threesomes with amateur bridge champions.

Maude took immediate control and hustled the boy to the bathroom where she removed his clothes to the bin and delivered some harsh scrubbing. When he was shining and appropriately scented with all traces of his previous abode exfoliated, wrapped up warm and asleep, she took the Judge by the hand and asked only if they could keep him. The cognoscente's meticulously prepared plan was redundant, never required nor heard, swept away in the rush of newly reborn maternal feelings.

When the boy was asked, the next morning, he said his name was Jessie but that did not suit her at all, not by a long chalk, 'Gerald, you shall be. A fine name. My Father's name,' Maude pronounced. And so, Gerald it was.

Gerald grew into his new life like he was born to it, fine clothes and fine food had him as happy as a pork butcher at a pig farm and as long as he kept M'Lady sweet, his life was sweeter.

She wanted him to talk properly so, elocution lessons were required. He dived in enthusiastically and was speaking, with proper diction and pronunciation, the Queen's English — Northern Irish style — as well as the Judge and his Lady in a month.

She wanted him to attend the local prep school. Tutors hired to bring him up to speed were glowing in their praise for his effort and achievements and speed of his attainments. Nobody said our boy was slow.

Maude deemed him ready and was about to burst with matronly pride as she presented her son to the headmaster at the start of summer term. He, believing some sort of adoption had taken place, did not bat an eye, especially as the Judge was a friend and benefactor.

Gerald quickly settled into his new routine and was a model pupil at his prep school and when at home a model son. Fastidious with his appearance, polite and urbane with both adults and his peers, he soon gathered around him a coterie of the most privileged scions of high society.

And all was well.

Gerald was thirteen when Maude and the Judge were first called to in to see the headmaster at the exclusive private school he now boarded at. This was the sort of place designed to make officers and gentlemen out of the upper middle-class boys surrendered to their care. The sort of place were headmaster, masters, teachers and governors were piously protective of the school's reputation. It seemed that there had been some sort of bother with another boy in the latrine.

After a deeply embarrassing consultation, it was decided that this should be excused away as 'experimentation' and blame fell on the other pupil who was a little older. Having this boy expelled solved the problem nicely — this time.

Things got out of hand however, and the headmaster had to have a soft word with the Judge at his chambers and most regretfully ask him to remove Gerald permanently. Maude was told that this was for theft, but the Judge knew the truth, and the fact that the boy he had ventured so much on had been giving blowjobs for cigarettes and ass for dinner money, disgusted him. It seems doing so for free and the favour of older boys was acceptable, provided it was at the right school with the right attitude. Hypocrisy was not something that bothered the good judge and his ilk at all.

Maude was distraught and so swiftly did her love turn to hate, helped on with a heaped spoonful of embarrassment that she could not even bring herself to speak to Gerald. In a scene reminiscent of Henry II, she called out to all and sundry, 'Who will rid me of this turbulent boy.'

Francis took the boy back to the whore house and had his driver threaten him with disembowelment if he ever showed his face near them or their environs again.

Jessie wasn't particularly bothered by this, he'd learnt a lot, had made contacts and had siphoned off a frankly astonishing sum from the old farts and was about to go into the movie business.

The Hospital

'Isn't it gorgeous, boys?' Jessie beamed at the trolls, standing back with his arms outspread.

'Best yet I'd say,' and 'Lovely lines boss.' Came the trollish replies from the corners of the room.

'God. I wish I'd a camera,' he said somewhat sadly, taking both chisel and hammer in one hand and bending down with his head at an angle to get a better view. 'Still. Mustn't complain. That was truly mind-fucking-blowing.' He handed the tools over to Troll Two who turned and tossed them into the toolbox.

He nodded at Troll One. 'Take this piece of shit somewhere and dump him. And you,' he said, grabbing my hair and lifting my head from the table, 'stop your fucking moaning and take the pain like a man.'

The little bit of me that was still aware mumbled, somewhat nonsensically, 'The way you take your dick!' and I'd never felt prouder of myself.

It didn't last.

They untied me and pulled me to my feet, the movement had me screaming again. He laughed, 'I've nothing against how a man takes his dick, in fact I'm often happy for two at a time, but this isn't a conversation,' he moved beside me and leaned in to shout in my ear.

'Now pay attention. If I see you again, I will kill you,' he said each word slowly, with emphasis, to make sure they penetrated my pain induced haze. Jesus why was I not unconscious. The last time I was blessed with concussion and a blissful lack of my condition — for the most part. Oh! for some of that bliss now.

They dragged me down the short corridor and out through the backdoor to an area outside, behind the pub. This was a small, cobbled yard leading to an alley that led to the street. It was full of crates of empty bottles and various other junk that bars recycle, reuse, store forever till they rot, and a wall fixed water tap above a metal drain.

They continued to drag me down the alley with the toes of my Gucci loafers sloshing through all sorts off muck and shit and out onto the main street. Not a care in the world. Fucking Philistines. I thought.

I dared to look at my hand as we passed beneath a streetlight and it resembled an inflated pink marigold glove with dark blue blotches and the strangest, almost beautiful, pattern of parallel, bright red lines — some bleeding a little, especially on the meatier parts of my palm and thumb — made up of the 10mm wide cuts from the chisel.

I grabbed my wrist with my good hand to try and stop it moving around but that was of little help as they opened the back doors of a scruffy white Ford Transit van and bundled me into it. The pain as I fell and banged my hand off the floor was indescribable. I curled up around my agony like a foetus and cared about nothing else.

After a few moments, the front doors opened, and they climbed in talking to each other in some sort of slang that I couldn't understand. This was littered with gestures back at me and accompanied with guttural laughter. The engine started and they drove far too fast down the cobbled street. The monstrous vibration that this set up in the metal floor under me was appalling and I vomited up my pain.

Things smoothed out for a short while, then it was if we were travelling across country on an unpaved road. The banging and bouncing eventually stopped and as the doors opened onto a dark street lit with flashes of flame and the roar of many angry voices, I became aware enough to dread what next was in store for me.

The lifted me by feet and shoulders this time, like they were carrying an already lifeless corpse and pushed their way through the mob till they reached a barricade made up of household furniture, tyres and two burning cars. Through the smoke and noise, I could make out the police and army in full riot gear on the other side of the barricade and just as we moved to the edge of the street a rioter beside us was snatched off their feet by a baton-round.

The thick rubber cylinder like bullet had struck the kid on the forehead and even as we rushed past to the kerb, I could see that he was dead. What is the world coming to? I thought for a moment. When a young teenage boy can't go out for a night of rioting and petrol bombing, taking his neighbour's goods by threat of force, and hijacking passing cars carrying folks home from a night at the cinema, without getting shot in the head by some spotty young paratrooper, desperately frightened and wishing he'd stayed in good ol' Engerland.

My thoughts were rudely interrupted as Ugly and the Beast tossed me by the side of the road into a filthy puddle by a blocked drain, and with a loving kick in the guts to say goodbye, disappeared into the haze leaving me retching.

The fun and games went on for another hour or so, punctuated by the dull crack of the baton-rounds from the army and the RUC. The seemingly joyous crowds massing at the barricades, leavened their taunting with crude petrol bombs and stones made from broken up flags were cheering gleefully whenever a police officer or squaddie was engulfed in flames.

Oh! the stamina of youth, that hour seemed an eternity to me before the armoured cars pushed the barriers aside, and the riot shielded police came rushing through to relieve their frustration with batons and the satisfying crunch of bone and the heavenly meaty slap of hardened wood on flesh.

I have often wondered about that moment. That moment when the Gold Commander decides enough is enough and unleashes his boys. There is always a certain amount of damage to goods, persons and property before they launch and break up a riot. Is this something agreed upon beforehand in some dark, smoke-filled room?

The army the RUC and a couple of the people's representatives in the form of the UDA or the RA blowing cigarette smoke and eyeing each other with hate, 'Youse can have one double-decker and two cars and as many tyres as you like. Three or four shops and half a dozen petrol bombs thrown. Then when everything is well alight, we'll hit you with ten or so baton-rounds…'

'Rubber bullets boss. Call it like it is for God's sake!'

'Ok! Have it your way. Ten or so rubber bullets, two, no, one to some raggedy-arsed fucker's bonce, then we and the boys of the great green army charge, mop up and we'll all be home and tucked up in bed with our cocks in our hands by sun-up. Agreed. Good! Out the back way as normal boys and we'll see you next week.'

I think I was most frightened then, curled up in the shadows in the lee of a small wall where I'd dragged myself. The rioters streamed past, the forces of good in pursuit. I thought that they might miss me lying there and pass me by, but the ambulance crews followed along some distance back and thankfully responded to my cries for help. And thus, I found myself in hospital again with the lights and the tubes and the reassuring beeps and the calm and comforting blue and white nurses.

In the hospital accident and emergency, they triage patients and send the urgent cases up for immediate surgery, up for the prep and the consultants, up for the instant intervention. It takes a great team with an Orthopaedic Surgeon and a Plastic Surgeon specialising in reconstructive surgical techniques, around four gruelling hours of intense concentration to put all the broken bones of the hand back together in such a way that you retain the use of it.

I got none of this.

The triage team booked me in behind some burn victims — overeager with the petrol bombs it seemed — and those with head wounds of various flavours — baton, baton-round, rifle butt etc. By the time I was on the table the no doubt, excellent and well-meaning surgeon probably wanted nothing more than some breakfast and a warm mug of coffee and as a result I awoke in the somewhat familiar surroundings minus a hand, missing a manus, without fingers, thumb and palm, cut of at the wrist and in not a little panic.

The Bedroom

The storm was doing its very best to break the spine of the sycamore and ash and the branches whipping about like dervishes were throwing wonderfully weird shadows on the window above our heads in the moonlight.

Marriage had changed nothing — as all the best marriages do. However, that cannot be said of pregnancies. God! But that is a hard old row to hoe. Even worse for the mother I discovered.

Lying on her back and feeling fat and grumpy, she was giving me some grief for having the temerity to sleep while she could not. Marvellous things were being said and although I was doing my best to let them slide off me like elephant shit off a hippo's back, the odd one got through.

'Why the fuck did I let you spout your far too potent semen into my fragrant maiden lady hole? Why can't you have tiny little crippled tadpole sperms, crawling about with their Zimmer frames, unable to swim and just dying with the effort and then running down my thigh. In fact, why did I even let you put your skanky little narwhal bone of a fucking penis anywhere near my gorgeously fertile girly womb?'

She groaned and turned over on her side for a moment, before sighing with frustration and rolling back onto her back.

'Fuck. Fuck. Fuck, Fuck, Fuck! Get out of me, you parasite! Sher! Go get a fucking carving knife I can't take this shit any more.'

I think it surprised her when I jumped out of bed and went

down to the kitchen.

When I returned, she looked at me nervously for a moment until she saw that I was carrying a basin half-full of warm soapy water and some towels. I set the basin by the end of the bed and pulling the quilt from her, grabbed her by both ankles and dragged her to the bottom of the bed so that I could let her feet fall into the water.

After I had washed and dried her feet, I massaged them with a little baby oil and then thinking she had fallen asleep, gently squeezed in beside her and closed my eyes. Not a chance, the ache had just gone from my relaxed eyeballs when she said, 'They say that sex can bring on the baby, but I'm too blissful to move. Do you think you could manage without leaning on me?'

'I'll give it a go,' I said. 'At least my potent sperms can't hurt you now.'

Sometime later, hoping to drift off but struggling with her arms across my chest. I heard her say, muffled from where her head was tucked into my neck, 'Sher, tell me a little more about your life, you know, just the mundane things, family things. Mummy and Daddy and little Sher on holidays, stuff like that.'

'Okay then. A man goes into a bar with a loaf of bread, a pound of liver and an erection.'

'Sher, stop being a tosser,' and she gently nipped my left testicle.

The Family Holidays

At ten I realised that we were luckier — if you want to call it that — richer, if you prefer the facts, than most of our neighbours. For instance, my father always rented a house near the beach, in one of the little seaside towns on the Ards peninsular for the whole of the school summer holidays. My brother and I would end up more like the locals than the itinerant day traveller or weekenders, calling them names and shouting at them to F off home, back to their city slums etc.

'You realise I'm just talking about the other boys. No innocents involved, no fathers, mother or girls.'

'Mmm,' she hummed into my neck.

Eight glorious weeks in shorts and bare feet, skin bronzed and hair bleached by the sun we lived liked beach tramps and avoided going home as much as possible. At night we'd huddle round the driftwood fires we made, cooking pieces of bacon on the end of a stick and heating our baked beans in the embers. Just occasionally mother, or father if he was there, would fail to find us and we'd wake up with the rise of the sun, covered in sand and freezing, to run home and face their wrath.

After he was murdered it didn't seem right somehow to go to the beach, so for years we ended up renting a cabin cruiser on Lough Erne. This became my father's new passion, as a result of which we rented at Easter, whatever the weather, and often twice more during the summer, usually the first and last week of the school holidays.

It should be noted that we were just about the only local family that did this. The vast majority of other 'crews' were German salted with occasional Yanks and French and once — a beautiful year — the Italians.

All through the bad, black days of the Troubles/Struggle these exotic people would come from far flung places to the lough and at least twice a year we met them.

I remember so little of those days now other than a sense of peace and calmness. This was one of those situations that by default separated my parents and that may have had something to do with my recalled sense of wellbeing.

In the first place, he was stuck behind the wheel driving the boat, except when he let me do it but with him tucked in tight to watch me, and she could sit on deck, far away, or down in the cabin, far away, or dropped off to do a bit of shopping, far away, or even forced into a spa at a shoreside hotel while we topped up the boat, far away.

When we tied up for the night things could get a little heated, especially as she insisted with no argument from us, that as it was a holiday she wasn't cooking, and we would eat at a pub or hotel close to the jetty. This, of course, meant drink taken and I would have to try and fall asleep to the tune of seemingly endless bitchy comments.

But it felt like the sun shone a lot. Boat tied up, my father and I would take the dinghy and row off fishing. Hours would pass and barely a word would slip our lips. Hands held out were filled with the right gear at the right time. Spot picked out to moor was met with no comment as was the unhitching, when a look to the sky meant, and was silently agreed with, that it was time to go back. Bliss.

She always refused to clean and cook the fish that we

brought back, and I know that is a sexist thing — assuming she would — for why couldn't I or my father do it? All I can say, is that it was different times, roles were much more fixed then. Anyway, I think the reason was much more to do with her trying to discourage us from fishing than any innate objection. Our loss was much to other's gain. The Germans, French and the beautiful Italians snapped up our catch, especially the eels for some reason.

With delight, a few words of broken English and a lot of arm waving, they would offer money, real spending money for anything that ended up on our hooks and in our boat.

'Why do I think that there were young women on that Italian boat?' Karine muttered at my shoulder.

It was all pretty staid really. I mean the first year he rammed the boat into a 'hidden' mud bank in the middle of nowhere, and I had to row my mother three miles to the nearest jetty so that she could walk another two miles to a public phone in order to call the boat yard to come and tow us off. I still remember the long, long, long row back to the boat. Jesus! I don't think she drew breath and every sentence started with 'your father this' and 'your father that'. An eleven-year-old boy shouldn't have to hear all that.

He'd stayed with the boat, to keep the pirates away, I assumed, and was bright as a daisy praising me for the way I'd managed the trip. I said nothing, just retired to my cabin and tried to shut out the echoes of her voice in my head.

The second year I had to be rescued by the Fermanagh Mountain rescue team.

'On a lake?' Karine snorted, incredulous.

'Yes, well not quite,' I replied.

We'd stopped at a place called Knockninny — nothing there — but close by was an old, abandoned quarry with steep cliffs and forest. I shouted to the bickering parents that I'd be a few hours and wandered off and had a great time. However, I had no watch, and it took much longer than I thought to get there and get to the top of the cliffs. When I had managed it, I realised that things were quickly moving towards twilight.

I was twelve now and a man grown, so I thought. A veteran of lake and river, an experienced explorer of woods and forests and of mountains and cliffs. I was going to be fine, but I wasn't going to try and climb down in the swiftly coming dark.

I found a nice tree with a nice niche and made myself as comfortable as I could. Not a thought for what must have been going through my parent's minds. I just assumed that they would know I'd be okay and would be back in the morning. Not a bit of it.

My mother would have called out the bomb squad if she could have persuaded them to join in the search with the RUC, the Lifeboat service and the aforementioned Fermanagh Mountain rescue service.

I have wondered often whether this was genuine concern about me, about my welfare, or was it simply for her the possible undying shame of having lost all her off-spring to misadventure. How could she hold herself as the epitome of motherhood in her church, offering sage advice to the younger women trapped unknowingly in the church's grey widow's web, if she became childness, an un-mother.

I was awoken, a torch shining in my eyes to heroic shouts of 'We've found him', wrapped up in survival blankets, tied to a stretcher and rappelled down the cliff in full view of the many search lights and all and sundry news reporters desperately hoping for a body — preferably a nicely smashed up one — to help promote their copy to the front page.

Jesus the noise the press made, the headlines. It took me years to stop hearing about that in school.

The third year, well the third year, the beautiful year of the Italians, nothing much happened except on my last day as we were bringing the boat into its home dock. I valued myself quite the seaman now, flinging the cabin cruiser about and manoeuvring into the tightest spaces at jetties and piers with flare and abandon.

We had managed to end up in the same place as the Italians for four nights in a row. Either they arrived first and we followed or the other way around. Nothing arranged, at least not that I could see. Perhaps it was the fish.

Marissa was her name, and she had that dark olive Mediterranean complexion and very dark brown eyes and I thought myself in love. She loved our fish, had barely a word of English and of course I had no Italian, but we had a great time. There seemed to be about ten of them on their boat and all did the instant bidding of the tiny bundled up grandmother. Not sure if she approved of me but she didn't shout at Marissa when I was around.

Anyway, last day. It had been raining all morning and was still drizzling as we brought the boat in. I was eager to see her and was at the front ready to jump off and tie the boat up — with a flourish of course. They had parked nose in, and the rear of their boat was flush with the short side of the jetty. We were coming in parallel with the long side and would end up at right angles to their stern.

I can only say that it was my excitement that made me forget just what a slimy slippery bastard those wooden planks get to be when they've had a coating of rain. Marissa was standing back a little with her parents further up towards the shore and the little

Nonna was on the back deck of their boat waving as we approached.

I leapt off when we were an impressive — to me — distance from the jetty and barely slowed down as my feet went out from underneath me. I could just see a little 'Oh' shape form in Marissa's mouth as I thumped down on my arse and skidded along the greasy wooden planks. With a sense of hopelessness, I put my hand down to slow my momentum and it simply slid into the gaps between the beams where it jerked me into a spin, broke my wrist, and thumped me into the stern of their boat. There was a despairing high-pitched squeal as her Nonna over-balanced and fell into the freezing cold, murky water.

I sat up wracked with pain, holding my wrist and not a little surprised to find absolutely no attention was being paid to me, all hands were scrabbling to extract an indignant, sweary and half-drowned, tiny old Italian lady from the lake.

When I came back from A&E with a cast on my wrist, I was told that they were packing up to leave. I knocked on the cabin roof to try and say goodbye to Marissa, but the father came out and started the engines, and as their boat pulled away from the jetty, said with a gesture and some Italian something that might have been, 'I'm sorry son, with young people leaving is painful. It's much better this way.' But I doubt it.

'Poor little old Granny,' Karine said with feeling, 'and what happened on the beach?' she prodded.

'Look you wanted to hear about my boring family holidays and I'm trying to explain that they usually went to shit, they aren't deeply interesting and meaningful,' I paused and moved my arm from under her, 'I mean who has a Christmas where you end up with two black eyes before lunch — one from each parent.' I gestured with both hands and paused again and just to play with her, 'Well the beach.'

After 'Italian' year my father surprised me by taking a house in Portavogie for the summer. I should explain that he would stay at home and go to work as normal and only come down for his mandatory two-week break, which meant, that in the absence of my sibling, I was effectively alone with my mother for six weeks. Fuck that! my fourteen-year-old self said and got a job.

By day I'd work in the local chip shop come café as a kitchen wallah and at night I'd hang around on the beach with some work colleagues — who were much too old for me but were willing to tolerate me even to the extent of the odd slurp of beer or drag of a fag. Then slump home, listen to the rant from mother about my loutish and inconsiderate behaviour and head off to bed to sleep late and arise just in time to head to work at eleven the next morning.

This worked extremely well, except for Sundays of course, when I had to trail along with her to the local Presbyterian church for both morning and evening services. I'd try very hard not to fall asleep but invariably I'd get an elbow in the ribs to wake me up and stop me snoring. Then a talking-to in the foyer before the inevitable tea and tray bake get together afterwards with the grey brigade. Deserved punishment, I can hear the Lord say.

I was doing table service on weekends when the café was busy and one Saturday while serving two nice looking girls, I couldn't help but notice their American accents. Now this was a very exotic thing and intrigued me; what brought these two, obviously well-travelled girls, to this place. I happened to run into them when we were closing up to find that they had been dragged to this lovely little rustic town by the sea, or dump, depending on your viewpoint, by well-meaning parents, and were looking for something to do. Desperately hoping it wouldn't backfire on me, I took them to the spot where the older peeps hung out and was in luck when I was hailed and welcomed.

I saw them as much as I could over the next week and I was getting warmed up towards one or the other — actually I couldn't have cared less which one eventually succumbed to my charms, just as long as it was one of them — indiscriminate teenage boy hormones.

I had gotten someone to buy me a bottle of cider and we went back to their rented but magnificently empty bungalow one afternoon. The cider drank, a game of strip spin-the-bottle was commenced. Now I'm normally good at spotting things that are off but blinded by cider and the not too gentle urging of those aforesaid hormones, I missed it, and not much later I'm in just my underwear and trying to work out how they were still mostly dressed, and the bottle stopped at me again. 'Off, off, off they chanted,' and I frantically looked for a way out.

'Okay,' I said and got up to go into the kitchen. 'I'll be right back.' The cider now started to tell, perhaps activated by my moving, and having done its damage I was now able to set aside the panic and with a growing but undeserved sense of confidence was going to style it out. The plan was to take off the pants and use a towel, step into the room to give them a quick reveal before covering up my modesty once again, bullfighter fashion. I could hear them talking loudly but paid it no heed. Holding my towel with one hand I opened the door and stepped through with my eyes closed — for some reason — while pulling away the towel and saying, 'You win.'

There was silence and I opened my eyes to see a very large man with thinning grey hair and a beer belly standing over the girls. 'What the fuck are yee doin' yee wee pervert,' in the broadest Shankill Road, Belfast accent I'd heard in a long time. I stumbled over to my things and grabbed them and mumbled something like, 'We were just playing.'

'I'll play yee with my foot so far up your arse that you'll taste shit, you wee cunt! Get the fuck out!' He swiped at me but missed. As I ran through the door, leaving my underwear in his kitchen, I couldn't help wondering why he didn't sound American.

She was laughing at me again, but I was used to it by now, 'Jesus Sher. The younger you, is always getting your wanger out. Should I be worried? Are you over it yet? Am I going to get a phone call from the police telling me to come down to the station to collect you after you've waggled your dangly goods at the old ladies at the bus stop?'

'That's all I am to you, aren't I? Just a figure of fun, just a dupe and a dope?'

'And the father of my child,' she laughed again. 'They were taking you for a ride, weren't they, well not for a ride to be precise.'

'Yes, but.'

I ran into the girls and their girlfriends at the tourist shop and had to endure their laughter amidst the beach balls and the buckets and spades. All that pointing and whispering into each other's ears then the staring and the giggling. No sign of any American twang now. I threw the flip-flops I was buying back into the box and ran outside and down the street into the alley behind the café. I looked up and saw the Other heading towards me. 'Wait a minute,' she called. 'Please.' I stopped and waited for her.

She came and faced me where I was leaning back against the wall and explained that it was all a joke that had gotten out of hand. She had wanted to tell me after the first time we met at the beach, but her sister wouldn't let her. She looked up into my eyes from under her fringe with her head bowed and told me that her and her sister were on their way home and that she actually kind of liked me. She was very sorry, and she'd like to make it up to me. She stepped closer and kissed me, gently at first, and then one of those early day, inexperienced, slobbery ones, all rushing and saliva, and then she took my hand and placed it on her hip and while holding the kiss slid it up to her breast.

'Linda Blythe,' I said, somewhat proudly, though Christ knows why.

Karine smiled, 'That's my naughty little sheriff,' and there was that warmth in her eyes.

'Right. Some sleep I think,' I said and rolled over.

'Not so fast sunshine,' she said, as she pulled me back by my shoulder, 'What about Christmas?'

'Look, I understand that you're looking for mundane family stories where happy parents love each other and their offspring, and their offspring love them back, but my lot are just as bad as any. Oh! I suppose that there must have been a time when they cared for each other, but it broke down a long time ago, even before I was born if I heard it right. Then they did that stupid thing of having another baby — me — to save their marriage. What sort of imbecile thinks that'll work?' I sighed.

'More than you'd think,' she replied softly.

'Okay then, one last boring Christmas family tale,' I pulled her arms over my chest again, 'and then sleep.'

Matthew had been dead for just over a year and we were approaching our first Christmas without him. I think, in hindsight, that unresolved issues over his death raised at the anniversary in November rumbled on. No one was really interested in Christmas, couldn't give a frig, and it showed.

My main present was a plastic rifle, a copy of an American M16 with some realistic bullets. I assumed they wanted me to commit suicide by army sniper. Fuck me! Not three months earlier a kid playing with a plastic rifle was gunned down by a green army solider in the twilight of a Ballymurphy evening. I had thought them banned.

He gave her a bread maker and a globular glass paper weight, inside which was a little glass sphere of the earth. She gave him a Gunn and Moore cricket bat, a beautiful thing of oiled willow and sensuous shape. He didn't play cricket.

After the gift exchange and long before the turkey (small) ended up in the bin they took to drinking, he in his shed in the garden and her in the kitchen. I tried some target practice in the front room, the room that was kept clean and pristine should a visitor call but was quickly told to take that bloody thing outside. Not a snowball's chance in hell I thought, never going to happen, no death-wish here, and went to read in my room.

An hour or two passed and a somewhat drunken mother shouted at me to go and get my good for nothing bastard father from the garden in for dinner. This was a surprise, both drunkenness and swearing, what would her God think. And why couldn't she call him, he was just outside the kitchen window for Christ's sake.

I trundled down the stairs, stayed as far from her as I could when passing her in the kitchen and muttering about the injustice went out through the back door.

A Christmas eve tradition of my mother's was to spring clean the house — perhaps Father Christmas would stay over — and that included washing the bedding. Thus, numerous white sheets were hanging on the clothesline running down the middle of the garden path, up and down which, roamed the newest Irish test batsman, mumbling to himself and drinking from a small bottle of whiskey.

'She wants you in for dinner,' I shouted then realised he wasn't paying attention and walked towards him. 'She wants you in for dinner,' I repeated seeing his head come up and look at me.

'Bloody woman, bloody, bloody Christ withered, bitter bloody woman,' he said.

I started to walk back into the house but, thinking that I'd better make sure that he'd heard me lest the mother give me more grief, turned around just as he, on the other side of the sheet whacked it as hard as he could with his new bat. Glad I was that he was in his cups or he might have hurt me more severely. As it was, the tip of the bat caught me high on my cheek across my right eye socket and knocked me to the ground.

'Fucking pratt!' I said, 'watch what you're doing for God's sake!' and got up and ran into the house holding my hand to my rapidly closing eye.

'Watch your language!' was the only response that followed me in.

I came in through the back door still at the run and turned to face her across the kitchen table, she thinking I was he, half-blind with the drink, let loose the paper weight with all her might.

'Bloody useless thing. Just like you. Here have it back!' she screamed.

Sort of frozen in the headlights, I had time to go 'Wha.' before the orb hit me high on my cheek across my left eye socket.

This knocked me backwards into the freshly filled linen basket which crumbled under my weight and spilled me to the floor. I had this moment of madness where I was going to congratulate her for such a fine throw, a woman who literally didn't manage to hit an old barn door while throwing a dart once.

I untangled myself and got to my feet, now finding it difficult to see through either eye, stumbled past her and the Christmas repast sitting out on the table and on the way catching everything I could, including our turkey (small) and dragging it off into the bin and onto the floor.

'Fucking Christmas! Fucking joke!' and stormed off to my bed, tears just managing to squeeze out through the swollen mess of my eyes.

'You know, I've not been in many fights, but I did play rugby for years and those were the only black eyes I ever got in my whole life,' I said to Karine after a moment.

'Don't worry kid, stick with me and I'll see get your share,' she replied in her best Mae West accent.

We lay in silence for a couple of minutes with me holding my hands to my eyes, remembering the pain and empathising with my younger self.

'Sher, please don't go to sleep, stay awake and talk to me,' she said softly, holding her stomach and groaning. 'You're just about keeping me sane.'

'My father was offered first refusal in buying the cabin cruiser rental company, marina, stock and all, that we had used those many times, and I remember the excitement in his face as he told us. Animated like never before, he outlined the move to Fermanagh and the times to come spent on the water. He was practically jumping around like a little kid with delight. Hugging me and talking of endless fishing, lying in the sun after a hard day's work prepping the boats for our imagined myriad of visitors.

"But I could never leave my church," my mother said primly, and perhaps only I caught the cynical glint in her eye that accompanied it. His face fell apart like a broken sheet of glass as he turned from her. He never once mentioned it again in all the years since and we never went on holiday there again.'

Karine just hugged me for a while.

After a few minutes I decided that it was now or never. I propped myself on one elbow to look her into her eyes. Momentarily distracted by the weirdness of seeing another living being kicking the everlasting shit out of her insides.

'The time has come, no more evasion you foul mouthed little scamp, explain the fish-based swearing.'

The Fisherman

Her escape nearly failed because it was broad daylight and in just her shift it was obvious who and what she was, but she had learned from her previous attempts. She left the sanctuary of the hedges as soon as her heart stopped pounding and she realised that no one was following her. She headed around the outside of the main building trying to keep as small as possible and ran down the side of the chapel, where voices were still raised in song, to the outside door of the sacristy. She held her breath as she turned the handle and swiftly slipped inside. God, it smelled, it smelled of that awful incense they used, but even that couldn't quite cover up his smell — whiskey, smoke and body odour — she was nearly sick with the memory it evoked.

Looking around she saw a desk and chairs and two wardrobes, opening the first she saw it was filled with vestments and stacked communion vessels. The other was filled with altar linens and black smelly suits, which to choose?

Three days she spent in that room and in that wardrobe. She ate some communion wafers and drank a few sips of the wine but that made her feel stupid. She peed into empty communion wine bottles and had to shit in a corner of the wardrobe which she covered up with old linens and sprinkled with incense. No one came in looking for her.

She curled up, terrified, each time the priest and attendants came in to prepare for mass, but they never even opened that wardrobe door. Finally, at Wednesday noon mass she decided that enough time had passed, and she took one of the suits, rolling up the sleeves and trouser legs and slipped out the door.

It was a working day, but she only wanted to get to the farm outbuildings without being noticed. Her hope was that they would have been already searched by now and therefore safe. Once there she climbed the skinny ladder into the loft and hid behind the sweet-smelling bales of hay.

Climbing down the ladder in the dark frightened her as her feet couldn't easily find the rungs but once on the ground, she crouched by the barn door and looked around. There was a quarter moon and enough light for her to see and be seen so she kept well into the hedges and started walking. When the moon set, she took to the country roads, diving into the verges whenever the occasional car came by.

The heavy old priest's suit, was sodden from wicking up water from the wet grass and that had made her so cold she barely noticed the rain starting again. Despondent, she sat on the curb and shivered, waiting for the dawn and the inexorable return to the nuns' loving arms.

It was here at her lowest that she found herself remembering the night of her father's death, clearly and in fine detail. For the first time she saw in her mind's eye every action and movement as if in slow motion. She heard the sound of the scissors thumping into her father's neck together with the awful groan he made and her mother's distain as she sneered and walked out leaving her alone with a little brother and a blood drenched body.

Her rising anger warmed her, anger at her circumstance, at the nuns, at her mother and anger at the whole bloody world for not caring enough about the needs of a little girl and boy. And there, wet-through and freezing cold in the pitch dark on the side of a road in the middle of nowhere, she swore to herself that she would escape and that someday she would be safe and have the love of a family and never allow the world to treat her like that again.

As she stood up and started to walk, she spotted a faint light ahead and hoping that this might be some sort of sanctuary she broke into a jog.

The run-down cottage's first floor windows were boarded up and bricks had been cemented into the ground floor windows and doors to prevent access. The light was from a small bulb protected in a wire cage hanging at the concrete bus shelter on the path alongside. Gratefully she stood inside and immediately felt better to be out of the rain. Unfortunately, the wind was still sucking away her body heat, blowing straight at her from the open side facing the road.

After catching her breath, she decided to walk around the cottage and ploughed through the grass and nettles growing thickly at the back, trying not to fall into them when she tripped on hidden obstructions in the dark. All the entrances were blocked but she noticed that a chestnut tree had overgrown the property at the gable end nearest the bus shelter and hoisted herself up its branches for a better look. Sure enough, the wind constantly whipping the branches back and forth, rubbing the wooden slats boarding up the last window on the right, had broken through and left a gap she just might reach if she was brave enough to climb out to the branch's end.

The room was musty and damp, but she found an old tarpaulin on the floor and quickly stripped off the heavy wet black suit. Then, even though the tarp smelled and was filthy with mouse droppings, wrapped herself up in it, sat in a dry corner against the wall and fell asleep.

When she woke it was still dark and she jumped up and down

to ease the stiffness and the aches in her muscles. Dragging her tarpaulin with her, she climbed out of the window and eased herself back onto the tree limb and down to the ground. Settling herself with the wind at her back she set out again trekking down the road to the south.

Within the hour she was regretting bringing the old tarp with her for the weight was becoming more than she could bear. Deciding she was warm enough, now that the rain had stopped, she tossed it into a hedge and feeling light and free her spirits rose as she continued down the road. As the ghost of the rising sun lit the eastern sky, she caught the scent of the ocean on the breeze and as she crested a hill saw below her a small fishing town.

Now what shall I do? She thought.

Tired, dishevelled, dirty and soaked through but inexplicitly happy and full of hope for the first time in years, she wandered the little town in search of inspiration. At the harbour, a small road ran in each direction along the coast. Tiny one-storey fisherman terraced cottages lined these for a few hundred yards, facing out to sea and across the thin road from a beach strewn with small boats and nets and all manner of fishing paraphernalia. Choosing a direction at random, she wandered along studying them.

Some were worn and tired, some abandoned and partially reclaimed by weed and shrub, but some were immaculate and obviously well cared for. The last house was not only this but was painted a beautiful sky blue with glossy window and door frames picked out in a clean bright white. Attached to one side, instead of another house was a small, paved yard on which sat some fishing gear, a small iron table and chairs and a coil of very large rope.

She climbed into that coil and although it was tight, she could breathe and relax, no one could see her unless they came right up and looked in. She was out of the wind and starting to feel warm and comfortable and she fell asleep.

She was awoken by the clatter of an old-fashioned metal bolt being drawn and the squeal of a warped wooden door being dragged out of its frame.

'Madge! Looks like the night trawl has landed and we've caught us a smelt or maybe a joey, but I suppose we'd best chuck it back and get on, lots to do today and no time of it to be spared on the baiting. Forbye, I'll have me breakfast outside this bright sunlit morning, pancakes and oatmeal, so I will.'

She heard the rattle of plates and cutlery and stayed hidden but, after things had quietened down, she dared to poke her head out and spotting bread and jam still on the table, ran over and started stuffing her face. She heard a gruff sort of laugh behind her and turned to see a large white-haired man with a trimmed white beard, maybe sixty, still strong and lean but ruddy and weather worn.

He was leaning on the door frame and looked at her as she stood frozen with fear, then knocking his pipe against his palm, he called out, 'Madge! Tis nothing but a slip of a girl, a sprat at most, lost it seems, do us not a bit of harm to let her port a while, if she's a willin'.' He walked into the house but left the door open.

Anu, she called him, at his request, though everyone else called him Jack, Mad Jack McCandless. Madge was a beloved wife long dead, but an everyday participant in most of his conversations. She grew to love this man as much as she thought she remembered loving her father.

After a lazy summer learning how to fish, how to set up tackle for shore or pier or boat, how to clean and gut and fillet and how to handle the little skiff he owned in the seas around the town, she asked him about school. She loved the idyllic lifestyle but yearned to meet other kids and get an education not poisoned with the taint of overbearing religious corporal punishment. He grunted his gruff sort of laugh and grabbed his old shapeless hat from the stand and headed out for the afternoon.

In September, he took her to the local high school and passed her off as a niece visiting while her mother got her head together. Whatever they all took that to mean or whatever he had done or said worked and she was enrolled with many other kids in the first form.

She grew through her teenage years cared for and loved. She would come home from school to cooked meals and a comfortable warm bed. At weekends and holidays, she would accompany him, working hard for the mackerel or herring and bargaining like a professional on the jetty when they brought in the shellfish and lobster.

He never called her by her name, preferring sprat or little one or other endearments and not once in their long years together, did he raise his voice in anger to her.

He drank most weekends or when some old ship mate hove into town, but he was a happy drunk, prone to telling tall tales and singing sea shanties in his quiet gruff voice. When he would talk of people and things he disliked, he would do so with a certain salty rhythmic swearing and the use of their full name. It was a habit she rather enjoyed catching.

Two weeks after her sixteenth birthday he told her he was takin' a berth because that 'Douglas James McArthur, dogfish, dug-faced, dick-sucker.' had let his best mate down. A force nine caught them in the Irish sea and all hands were lost with the trawler.

A wizened, warped and withered old woman turned up a few days later claiming the house, Anu was her brother it seemed, and her somewhat sniffling, sneering off-spring, who was wandering around lifting things up and examining them, made it clear that there was no room for her any more.

She joined the Army Nursing Corps.

'He sounds like he was a lovely man. I'm sure you miss him,' I said softly, thinking of an eleven-year-old little girl-child, walking miles through the night in the dark and rain not knowing where she was headed or what she was headed to.

'I do. I think of him often. It's funny, but even though he never once embraced me or held my hand in an adult child way, I know that he loved me. I think he was wary of my reaction as if he knew what had happened to me and what the touch of a grown man might do. It was the same with my name, it was like that was the past that he never wanted to bring up. I felt safe like I had never done before.'

'Come here,' I said, pulling her to me and just hugging her for a while. 'You know I really like that. Can I use it? We'll have our grandchildren call me that, Anu, and I'll pretend to be a salty old sea dog. God I can almost smell and feel the ocean.'

'My waters have broken, you dick-head!'

138

The Hotel by the Sea

The tide was out. Far away from us the beautiful expanse of unmarked sand was just starting to attract the morning's first sea birds. The dawning sun sparkled off the smooth and peaceful sea like a spotlight in a mirror and we were most glad to see it, as we were huddled together and shivering now.

'Take me somewhere,' Karine said, brushing the hair from her forehead and some errant sand from her lips, 'Take me somewhere away from this shit. Somewhere where people won't kill us just because we want to listen to music.'

'I doubt that there is any dark corner of this tiny land that hasn't had the grim reaper's untimely visit. And I don't doubt that he waits there still, crouching in the terraced houses, the flats, the semi-detached and the villas. I see him in the pubs on the green side and the clubs on the orange side and he looks the same no matter where you land,' I said, teeth chattering. 'After all, we're a homogenous murderous society. No class or underclass undefiled by the long and evil reach of our freedom fighters/loyalists/terrorists.'

She sighed a little, and hugged her knees, 'Scotland, England, Wales?'

'The Scottish always want to know what side you're on because they're closet religious bigots. The English despise us all as 'Paddies' so that they can be sweepingly snobbish and arrogant. And the Welsh — well that would be a possibility if I didn't have to go to work on Monday.'

She shook me off and stood up, wobbling a little with stiff limbs, and running her hands down the sides of her body from her breasts to her hips she said, 'You'd give up a few days away with this to go to work!' then paused for effect. 'Fucking take me home.'

Frantically trying to think of something, I jumped up and reached out to take her by the shoulders, but she slapped my hands away and turned her head from me. Desperately striving through sheer will to make her look into my eyes, I started, 'L. L. Listen. I didn't mean that. I don't know what I was thinking, there's nothing else I'd rather—'

She finally turned her head to look at me. Those eyes afire it seemed, those sparks of green from which light seemed to shine in that mess of blue-black bruising, framed by the clouds of her hair blowing towards me on the breeze.

'I'm going to have so much fun, you're as easy to wind up as a kid's Yoyo.' Leaning in, she kissed me gently on the lips and said in that fake western accent she does so well, 'Come on Sheriff, let's blow this town.'

I took her hand and we turned to walk back to my bike, 'Now that I think on it, there is a place I know, a lovely cove with a pretty little hotel on the north coast that's quite quiet.'

'I bet you say that to all the girls,' she replied with that smile, 'let's git.' And we almost broke into a run with excitement and anticipation.

It was a strange thing. We were full of plaster dust and sand and although I would have loved to go home and change, the thought of doing so, of stepping back into the mundane, into the day-to-day reality appealed not in the slightest. I was on a huge adventure, skirting death with my beautiful co-star by my side and daring the world to do its best to stop us.

So, it did.

Some forty minutes later, we were coming into Ballymena, a small town on our way to Portballintrae and the delights of the lovely Bay Hotel and had stopped momentarily at a junction. The lights went green and I happened to glance left as we moved off, right into the eyes of a middle-aged man in a blue Ford Cortina waiting at the next side street. He seemed to keep eye contact with me as he pulled out, looking at me but completely blind to the fact that a motorcycle was approaching. We hit the front of his car and I had a fleeting vision of Karine flying over my head to hit the road ahead of me as I somersaulted over the car's bonnet. Something snagged at my leg as I passed, and I landed on my back on the tarmac.

I do not believe in God or in Fate or Karma, they all seem so ridiculous to me, but circumstance, circumstance on the other hand can be a right motherfucking bastard.

It, if you like, decided to fuck us up, but to add balance, it decided to leave us a clear road with no oncoming traffic. Its curse was to remove us violently from our little dream and its blessing was to drop us unto that road at 30 miles an hour, unpulped by any approaching car.

I tried to stand up and only then noticed the blood pissing out of my leg. Whatever I'd snagged had ripped open a worryingly deep, six-inch gash above my knee. I looked around for Karine and started crawling towards her as she sat up and pulled her helmet off.

'Fuck, but you know how to show a girl a great time!' she grinned.

Christ! This girl has some grit. I thought. Any other would be in bits by now, curled up and comatose, crying for their dear mother and wishing it all would end. She'd nearly been killed in a car bomb explosion, headbutted in the forehead by yours truly and now had the temerity to grin as she once again nearly died in a road traffic accident, and all within twenty-four hours. She made me want to step up to match her.

'Are you okay?' I asked, somewhat clenching my teeth as the pain started to bite.

'Fine and fucking dandy,' she replied, pulling herself over to meet me. 'Looks like you're leaking a lot.' She took her jacket off and with my help ripped the sleeve off her shirt which she tied around my leg over the wound. 'Press your hands down here,' she said, putting my hands on top.

Circumstance now skewed towards the generous, because being only two minutes away from the Braid Valley hospital, the ambulance arrived quickly, and after loading me in on a stretcher and helping her in beside me, we took off. However, even though I was beginning to feel a little woozy, I couldn't help but notice that we were going in the wrong direction. Karine held both my hands with hers, and, as we pulled into St. Patrick's barracks on the western edge of the town, home to the Royal Ulster Rifles, she said 'There's something I need to tell you.'

Karine was an army nurse! A member of the Queen Alexandra's Royal Army Nursing Corps and seconded to the Royal Victoria Hospital to offer some training on trauma injuries, on gun-shot wounds, to the nurses there.

My first thought was, 'How do they keep you safe?' worried and knowing that grabbing her and doing unspeakable things to the delicious body I'd just got to know would be quite the Irish Republican Army coup.

'They don't know, you lemon,' she said. 'As far as my colleague nurses are concerned, I've learnt my trade in the South-Central part of LA, drive-byes a twice daily occurrence, and not in Northern Ireland and the Falklands. I'm very good at keeping quiet and eventually people learn to respect your privacy. As long as I don't socialise too much with them and drink too much, I'll not spill the beans. Anyway, my time is up, I'm supposed to be moving on to the next thing and I was only out yesterday with them for a goodbye drink.'

'I seem to remember you pissed as a newt at my father's funeral,' I said, and then in amazement, 'and you were in the Falklands war?'

'Well, yes. And yes, then too, but that was someone's birthday party. Jesus, what's a little risk now and then — you fat little halibut,' she said, squeezing my arm.

'Remind me to ask you about that later, but what the fuck are we doing here?'

I was interrupted when the doors opened, and some orderlies helped her down and took her away. A few moments later they came back and wheeled me into what was obviously the medical centre — it said so on the sign — and into a curtained off partition. A uniformed man came in and introduced himself in a loud, unmistakably posh as a 1972 Range Rover covered in dog hair, Edinburgh accent, as Captain Richard Smethurst Colquhoun.

I replied with, 'Where's Karine. I need to see her and why am I here?'

'Do not worry. She is fine. Just getting a bit of a check-up, I'm afraid. She won't be long, I'm sure,' he lent down and peered at my leg. 'This little mess will need quite a few stitches.' He beckoned the orderly over, 'But nothing that Staff Sar'nt Bickerstaff can't handle, eh!' he stepped back. 'Carry on.' And marched away.

'B. B. but wait! Why am I here?' he continued walking and

ignored me.

'I'll gee ya a wee jab fer this laddie,' the Sergeant said and stuck a needle into my leg above and below the wound. Fairly soon everything from my groin down was numb and I watched with some sort of detachment as he cleaned away the blood and then stitched something inside my leg. He then folded back the flap of skin that had been ripped opened and sewed it back in place with a practiced verve. A final wash, then clean gauze and linen bandages and he was done.

'Can you tell me anything?' I asked.

'Nay laddie, not ma place,' and with that he walked away as well, leaving me alone.

I was shaken awake and a familiar voice said, 'Don't you look all sexy as the wounded hero. I've a fair mind to jump in there with you.'

'Karine! What the fuck is going on?' I croaked, 'and I'm numb from the waist down.'

'Has its advantages,' she smiled. 'Look, it's just procedure. If we're ever in an accident we tell the medical staff to take us to the nearest military base or call a certain number for a military response team and the army take over from there. The local folk were on the ball today though.' She explained. 'You're a civilian so this is as far as you can go. In fact, they normally wouldn't treat you at all, they should have taken you back to the normal A & E, but I suppose with things being quiet they decided to sort you here.'

'You're in the army. Why didn't you tell me?' I asked.

'You know damn well why,' she replied. 'Not the sort of thing to trust new people with, is it?'

'I suppose not. Now what happens?'

'An army ambulance will take us to the military wing of the

Musgrave Hospital for me to get looked over and signed out.'

'And me?' I asked.

'You'll have to come with me. Think of it as a bit of a pause in our plans.'

I looked at her and then down at my leg, 'It will be a few weeks before I'm jumping off any wardrobes.'

'Never understood that stupid joke,' she said. 'Here they come.'

Orderlies arrived and lifted me into a wheelchair and with Karine limping behind we went back out into the cold and into the waiting ambulance. This time it was a standard army camouflage painted one, obviously a generation older than its civilian sister.

I slept for the trip to the Musgrave, only waking up when the local anaesthetic wore off and the pain hit me. The Orderly gave me some pills and Karine held my hand until I went back to sleep.

There was a lot of to-ing and fro-ing at the military hospital until finally I was put in a civilian ambulance for the trip home. Karine pulled herself up beside me, 'Remember you're on a promise, so get better quickly,' she smiled that smile.

'Can't wait to see you on your back with your hands around your ankles.'

I imagined a little gasp but was not sure why as I'd said that to myself — hadn't I.

Being in military 'custody' I had not been allowed to inform anyone of my whereabouts — not sure why — and this meant that I had no means of countering the statement made to my mother by the RUC officer who called at the house. Maybe this echoed in a horrible way for her or maybe she was indifferent to my plight.

'You might have phoned me and saved me all this trouble,'

she said, positive as always, pointing to the people gathered in the front room and the heaps of sandwiches, cocktail sausages and other treats that formed the mainstay of family or social gatherings in those times. 'The man just told us that you'd been in an accident and that they didn't know which hospital you'd been taken to. I tried them all and since no one knew of you, Masie (the busybody from next door) said that you must be in the morgue.' Hard to tell if this upset or soothed her.

'I phoned your friend Door, Dour is it, and suddenly a bunch of hairy — none to clean if you ask me — bikers, turn up on my doorstep.' While she was letting me know how much I'd inconvenienced her, my friends had come into the hallway to see me, thankfully pushing her into the background. I could just hear her muttering, 'And with some floosy too. What will the neighbours think?'

The days passed and nothing was heard, until about three weeks later I answered a knock on the door. Friday evening, bound to be the paper boy or something looking for payment.

'Hey, Sheriff. Is that a six-shooter I see?' she purred, leaning on the porch in that same exact pose, all elegance and feline like, that I first saw at the church.

'Where the fuck have you been! Not a word, not a call. Jesus Girl. I thought you were dead!' I sounded far too much like my mother for comfort.

'Easy there, fella. Can I come in before you tear my head off?' and she brushed against me as I closed the front door. They say smell is the most evocative of the senses and I heartily concur. Just the lightest scent of her, her perfume, her skin, her hair, had me remembering everything of our short time together in the most glorious detail.

'Of course. Come on,' I said somewhat croakily, and led the

way into the front room still limping a little while my mother nearly broke her neck craning round to see who it was.

I closed the door on my mother's open-mouthed disbelief, and as Karine walked past me, she turned, fell into my arms and kissed me.

'You know what? In our somewhat wonderful, eventful time together we never exchanged numbers or addresses. I had to 'run into' Claire — the short blond one — and see if she or any of her friends had copped off with any of your mates, and still had an address. Thankfully, she was still seeing that friend of yours — Dour — what sort of a name is that anyway, much to her very rich and pompous parents delight and he led me here. So, let's get going.' She seemed so excited and alive and so much of what I'd been missing.

'What do you mean get going, get going where? I'm still hobbling about like one leg is shorter than the other and haven't been out of the house in a month,' I said moaning. Then, I suddenly realised that I'd done this to myself. All coped up with misery because she hadn't shown and depressed because I'd thought she'd dumped me.

'We have a date I believe. The Bay Hotel and something about my legs over my head,' she said, loud enough to be heard through a few thicknesses of door.

'Holy fuck!' I gulped. Just hearing that and the accompanying outraged gasp from my mother behind the door woke me up. I blushed and Karine looked at me with that smile on her face.

'Didn't think I'd heard that, did you?' she said.

'Nope, but in my defence — drugs taken,' now my mind was made up. 'Let's git.' My accent wasn't nearly as good as hers, but it served.

I opened the door and my mother nearly fell into the room.

'See you Ma. We're off for the weekend to Portballintrae,' I tossed back at her as I grabbed my stuff and helmets from the hall.

'You'll end up like your father, what with that floosy of yours,' she shouted at my back.

I had no idea what that meant but happily replied, 'I hope so.'

I was nervous on my bike for a short while and even more so when we approached the scene of our accident in Ballymena. I could even feel her tensing up from the pressure of her arms around my waist, but swiftly that fell behind us and just as quickly it was forgotten as we headed on to Portballintrae and the Bay Hotel.

Hotels were not exactly choc-a-bloc with visitors in those times, even in the summer, so not a raised eyebrow was evident as we rolled up in our bike leathers and lack of overnight bags looking for a double room. Instead, we were shown to a lovely bay-windowed room overlooking Portballintrae's beach and the coastal path winding through the dunes on either side. It was bright and modern and had a lovely king-sized bed that I was trying not to stare at.

The door closed and I felt a little nervous as if this were my first time alone with a woman.

'I think I'll have a bath,' I said. What the fuck! So much for being cool, calm and sophisticated.

'Okay, I'll join you,' she replied. Thank you Lordy.

I can't say that I'd recommend the situation. It was nice, then awfully awkward which resulted in a lot of water on the floor following by wet bodies on the bed — ankles, hands and all.

We managed to get down for dinner in the restaurant. We

were so relaxed and at ease with each other that I felt like I'd known her forever.

We seemed to be the only people staying in the hotel, so there wasn't any pressure to eat up and get up. They seemed to think that we were honeymooners such was the attention.

Coffee and cake time came, and I decided to bite the bullet.

'So, what should I call you, Corporal Nurse, Sergeant Nurse?' I ventured.

She gave a little rueful sigh, 'Second Lieutenant Nurse actually.' Then took a deep breath and said, 'I'm not good at talking about my past life Sher, and I hope that you are OK with that but since you were so kind to me, washing my back and making sure that I did my exercises, I'll make a small exception.'

I gulped my too hot coffee and manfully swallowed the pain not wanting to interrupt her.

'At sixteen I was living in one room in a rather dowdy three storey on the Ormeau Road, constantly having to avoid the scumbags that lived in the same house who thought of me, especially went drunk, as their personal female entertainment. I was going to the Belfast Tech to do my 'O' and then 'A' levels, working in part time jobs, and waiting patiently until I was old enough to join up. You had to be nearly eighteen then, and probably still do. I did my basic training and then my nursing degree in Birmingham and then started work in various bases and hospitals around the country.' She paused and sipped her coffee.

'Everything was fine and going well and I was enjoying myself, but the Argentinians invaded the Falklands, and I was posted. I and a few others were assigned to HMS *Ardent*. After the initial attacks, when it was bombed the first time, we were sent ashore and I stayed there until the cease fire.

I was recommended for Officer Training and when we got

home, I went up to Sandhurst and passed out as a Second Lieutenant. The night I met you I had just decided to resign my commission and become a civilian nurse.'

She moved her seat around the table a little so that we were side by side and within thigh touching distance, 'Enough of that gloomy stuff, is there a nice beach for a late evening walk?'

God! There was so much more to that story, but I'd need to be patient, 'Yep. A lovely long strand and the moon's out.' I signed for the bill and we collected our bike jackets from the room and headed down to the beach.

It was a beautiful night, but I think by then I'd consider it beautiful if it was three degrees under and blowing a sleet filled gale in my face. The moon was bright, and the sea was calm with that gentle susurration of the waves running in on the beach. There were other couples around with the same idea, but we steered clear and headed along the path towards the dunes. I was even comfortable holding hands in public, so content was I, and I thought I'd reciprocate a little in an attempt to draw her out a bit further.

'I had a friend who joined the Royal Ulster Rifles as a boy soldier. I say friend, but he was a strange kid. He used to crow at the dawn like a cockerel and wake everyone in the street and he was just about the only person I ever had a fight with. Technically three fights.'

'Oh! Do tell,' she said, grabbing my arm and pulling in tight. We stepped down off the path unto the sand and headed for the ocean.

'A bit boring really but he liked me — Christ knows why — and was forever trying to get me to go places with him. This one evening he was chasing some girl he fancied, and he asked me to be his wingman when we got to the local youth club — in the church where you made such an impression on my mother.'

'Happy to help out,' she said.

'We get there, and I swear he must have planned this whole thing in his head in advance because he drags me aside and says to follow his lead, to do what he says no matter what. We go up to the girls playing darts, and he jumps in, grabs the darts from the board and tells the girls that he is going to be a live target while I throw. This is obviously meant to impress them so much that they'd fall into his arms moist thighed.

They laugh, but not in a good way, and he hands me the darts and tells me to throw them at the board over his head. "Are you out of your fucking mind," I say, but he is undeterred and takes up his place at the dart board, a good three inches under the bullseye, and waves me to the oche.

I must admit that I was bricking it. What was he on? I hadn't thrown a dart in weeks and I'm sure that I meant to hit all those fives and ones.

I remember vividly to this day, and in great detail, the flight of the dart. He was standing there, all expectant because this was going to make his name and I could see him making googly eyes at the girl he wanted, sure that in just a few seconds she'd be like putty in his embrace. The flights were a bit worn, a dull red, and the barrel was scratched and faded from its once shiny silver. I watched it fly from my hand towards the bull in a nice arc and was certain for a moment that all would be well.

It wasn't so much a clunking sound, but it was more that, than hitting a melon with a hammer.

He did a little skip forward as he brushed the dart from the top of his crown where it had landed, penetrated and sat up like a corner flag. He stormed out past me, blood pouring down his face and ran home. He said not a word to me until he came back from America some six months later with a flick knife he had bought and wanted to show me.

One thing led to another — as it always did with him — and we ended up stabbing each other.' I held up my wrist so that she could see the scar where his knife went in.

She had stopped laughing and asked, 'Is his bigger than yours then?'

'The stupid bugger wouldn't let me take him to get some stitches, went to bed without sorting it and his mother found him in blood drenched sheets an hour or so later and had to rush him to A & E.'

'Do you still get together to bleed each other?' she smiled, as we turned and headed back to the path.

'No. He's dead,' I said. 'He stole some television cameras from a TV studio in Manchester — I'm sure that it made sense to him — and this gave him grandiose visions of becoming a gangster. Of course, this was all after his dishonourable discharge for clocking some officer who kept calling him odd-ball. The world can be quite hard on those of us so challenged.

He wandered around Belfast with a couple of minders pretending he was Al Capone for a few months, constantly offering me a job but never saying what it was, until he ran afoul of some real gangster in the UVF from Newtownabbey who cut his nuts off and left him to bleed to death.'

'Jesus Fuck!' she said, 'he sounded harmless.'

'He was. As long as you avoided him at dawn or with darts or flick-knives,' I replied.

'Come on I'm feeling the need to be warmed up, with some stretches perhaps,' she said, with that smile that did its butterfly thing in my stomach.

As we walked past the reception desk the *maître d'hôtel*

called out that there was a phone call for me. I went over to the desk and he handed me a phone and when I hung up, I turned to Karine a little pale.

'My mother has died.'

The Solicitors

The solicitor's office was a little musty from the beige folders stacked, bursting to the seams with papers, on every possible surface, even those parts of the floor not used for normal foot traffic had their waist high islands of folders or papers bundled with red thread. For all that it had a lovely, wood-panelled ceiling and wainscotting in what looked like a rich glowing cherry and stylish, well-worn but still sumptuous red leather seats.

He was a small, precise man, with a greying comb-over and a wrinkled, black pin-striped suit. There were orange nicotine stains on the fingers of his right hand and the tang of cigarette smoke still clung to him though I could see no ashtrays.

I had buried my mother after enduring another ludicrous service at her church, during which I became convinced that if every speaker were speaking true, my mother was Mother (soon to be Saint) Teresa of Calcutta. There was one beautiful moment during his eulogy, when the minister looked up just before the 'Amen' and saw who was sitting at my side. A wonderful instant when he blanched and nearly choked on his words. What a lovely metaphor that would have been had he expired in front of the congregation, and I fervently hoped that he would be apprehensive just before every 'Amen' of his career to come.

Things went on for far too long both there and at the cemetery. I had arranged tea and cakes in the church hall, just as she would have liked, and received the condolences of the grey widows there. That left only a few of us to endure the minister's drawn-out sermon at the graveside. The cynic in me suggested that he was doing so on purpose just to piss me off, but how would that be; a man of the cloth being petty and mean spirited — never happen.

I buried her beside my father and swore to him that I would have him exhumed and burnt and scattered as he had desired, his ashes thrown to the fresh offshore wind, and splayed on the restive sand to be dispersed on the boundless ocean.

I had drifted off a little arranging that in my head and missed what the solicitor had been saying, 'Sorry, could you go back a bit, I didn't quite catch that.'

His desk, although stacked with files at the extremities was made of the same cherry wood as the wainscotting and was probably contemporary. It was much too big for him and may well have fitted a bigger personality in days gone by. The silver gilt service sitting on the red leather inset had been brought in by his creaking and pensionable secretary, but I had left the tea and dried raisin cake untouched.

'Why yes, of course, it can be hard to hear sometimes and even harder to take in,' he said. 'I was reading from your late mother's will and explaining that she has left her estate to her church.'

'What? All of it?' I said, not that I really cared, I didn't seem to feel about money the way most people did, never had fantasies about being rich, owning super cars, jets or yachts.

'Why yes. All of it,' he answered solemnly, as he put his hands precisely on each side of the document on the desk in front of him and looked up at me.

'Right. Well, I'll get out of your way,' I replied, a little snippily. 'Not entirely sure why it was necessary for me to be here and get that slap in the face in public,' as I started to rise from my seat.

'Why yes, of course, no need at all really… other than your father,' he said, as he reached for another document to his left. I sat down again and decided to take a sip of my tea after all.

'You are confusing me now, Mr. Clemence-O'Reilly, what are you talking about?' I said, in somewhat of a muddle.

'Why yes, your father it would seem was highly prescient,' he gave a little dry, nearly suppressed, giggle. 'He inserted a 'Survivor Clause' into his own will. In which he stated that should your mother post decease him, within a period not to exceed one calendar year, his estate should fall entirely to you,' again with little dry, nearly suppressed, giggle.

'Excuse me Mr. Clemence-O'Reilly, but I am at a loss to understand the humour in this,' I said and wondered where in the hell that pompous little *bon mot* had come from.

'Why yes, surely not my boy,' he said, 'I was not a great fan of your mother but considered your father a friend — we had many a jolly night together laughing at man's folly.'

I was struggling with that image but let him carry on while I tried the cake and then immediately looked for a way of spitting it out without him noticing.

'Why yes, my likes or dislikes have absolutely nothing to do with the execution of my duty and I would have seen your parent's combined estate settled to the church post haste. However, it is certain that your father's wishes will be upheld, and I hope, why yes, that it sets, at least partially, against your mother's clear desire to spite you. The spiter spit, if I may twist the idiom to humour's cause,' yet a third little dry, nearly suppressed, giggle.

He continued, 'There are some funds in pensions and the like amounting to around £50,000 after taxes and duties and so on.

156

And may I suggest, why yes, that you leave those and your mother's liquid assets to the church. This should forestall any attempt to challenge the will.'

'Why yes,' I said, 'that seems most reasonable.'

He didn't even flinch.

'Why yes, now let us turn to the family home,' he carried on. 'Once again your father's wishes in this take precedence and if you wish me to arrange a sale at best price, I'm happy to undertake that for you with alacrity.' He removed his glasses and polished them with a little cloth taken from his inside pocket, looking up at me and waiting on my response.

'I think that's the way to go,' I said somewhat sadly. 'I can't see myself returning to, never mind living in, that house.'

He replaced his glasses and hesitated a moment looking down at the document before him as if finding his place. 'Why yes, that leaves the lands and house at Beechfield. Which are also yours as of today and the keys of which I have somewhere on my person.' He proceeded to rummage through his pockets and failing to find anything, he opened and closed drawers on his desk until he unearthed a standard door key attached to a cream-coloured label.

'Your father was very proud of that house and built it with his own hands, as indeed you must know, why yes. It was my understanding that it was his desire to divorce your mother and live there in peace. Though I must here now confess, why yes, that he never actually gave voice to same.'

'Jesus! Mr Clemence-O'Reilly,' he glanced up at me with censure. 'A house. Lands. Divorce. Jesus!'

Again, the little moue of censure. Enough to throw him off his 'Why yesses'. 'Your father confided in me. He was miserable in his marriage but determined to stay so until you had flown the nest. He had probably made this decision shortly after your birth, but he had also decided to do something about it, in preparation if you will.

I know that he bought the land long ago, perhaps with another dream in mind. Forty acres in the hills near Moneyreagh together with a decrepit farmhouse. It was evidently a bargain so shortly after the war, but he let it lay fallow and it was slowly returning to nature.

It was around the time of your late brother's demise that he returned to it. He knocked the old stone-built house down and slowly dug the foundations, put up the walls and roof and fitted it out. It was a labour of love and I have had the great good fortune of seeing him come alive in that place.

The land he tended as a good Shepherd should, planting groves of chestnut and oak, elm and birch, creating and enhancing the hedgerows with hawthorn, sycamore and ash, forming long and twisting bridle paths along the borders and through the copses and glades, and setting weirs in the stream to create wetlands and ponds.

My understanding is that he has gone to his rest leaving the house finished but for one room. I believe he has left the kitchen undone, perhaps that was too final a step, perhaps a complete house would have precipitated a decision. Perhaps it was left undone as a metaphor or perhaps he was hoping against hope for some input. Whatever his reason, he chose not to share it with me, but it is my fervent wish and I trust, if I am not exceeding the bounds of my service, that you will finish it with the love and care he devoted to the rest of the house.'

'Wh. Of course, I shall,' I said dumbfounded, 'but divorce. It just doesn't seem like him.'

'Why yes,' he was confidently back on track, 'we are not

given to know another's mind and although I fear he was living a life of quiet desperation, it was not in him to be petty. He was going to sign over the family home to your mother as well as a very generous stipend, much more generous than any court would have awarded, I feel.'

He took off his glasses again and wiped them with the small cloth from his suit pocket, pausing once more as if unsure of his next words.

'I should not, but cannot help, compare your mother's response to these revelations. She sat right where you are sitting and got rather heated, why yes, heated. Wanted the land and house at Beechfield gone, sold at auction as if it had never been, why yes. It is only, forgive me if I appear unkind, her timely demise, that has saved it for you. Still these matters are now moot, things have settled as they have, and we must move on.'

'Thank you,' I said, standing as I picked up the key he had set on the desk. 'What strange turns the world takes.'

'Why yes, indeed it does,' he said, putting on his glasses and rising to show me the door. 'My secretary will furnish you with some paperwork and addresses etcetera, and please be assured that I remain at your service as once I was at your father's.'

Jessie

A young man without a sense of morals can do well in a moral society. Especially in a nominally strait-laced Presbyterian one or a fervent Catholic one. A young man who had seized his opportunities to learn, when he had the chance, the weaknesses, vices and desires of the ruling elite. Their innate need to be shorn of their religious hair coats and catechisms. Their yearning for something of the flesh, denied to them in this life and certainly not available in any heaven proffered by their churchmen.

Jessie grew to adulthood in a seedy environment taught to serve the occasionally feral longings of a number of clients. He endured their demands and quickly learned that having a stable cohort of favourites lessened the overall work rate and associated risk of damage.

He became a steady earner and impressed the Madame on whom he was once again dependant, suggesting certain live shows and delighting in their success. With her help and contacts and of course her enthusiastic staff, who saw this as a way to make more money per dick suffered, as it were, his nascent film production company blossomed.

Not being the sharer type, Jessie resolved his first business crisis in the same way he was to resolve all future problems and the wielding of that power left him with a high, unmatched by any drug, drink or physically contact.

Madame had gotten a little too greedy, asking for a greater and greater portion of the proceeds. Indeed, much of it was going up her nose, as her liking for the newly fashionable cocaine was becoming endemic.

Now Jessie was a cross party, all religion-inclusive businessman and he thought about who might solve this for him for a long time. His chosen target, a Brigade Commander with the Shankill UVF and a lay preacher with the church, model citizen etc. understood the implicit blackmail straight away in Jessie's request for a favour. While agreeing to his demand he did, however, present Jessie with a warning.

'People in this life will stand to be squeezed a little, son, but squeeze too much or too hard, and you'll end up with all the juice coming out of *your* head,' the man said. Jessie took that to heart and held it dear for the rest of his life, massaging never squeezing, whenever the situation required.

In this particular case, the bomb they placed to destroy Madame du Barry's was made to look like the work of the IRA, which made the Commander pleased and got him brownie points with the other Belfast UVF Commanders. Jessie was elsewhere, in his new apartment overlooking the river when it went off. The timing was unusually early for these things, in mid-afternoon before they were open for business, but that been implicit in Jessie's instructions. Madame and all six of the girls present burned with the building but nobody cared much, they were just whores.

After that, there was no stopping him. Delightful films, both imported and home grown, implements of pleasure and light torture, costumes and bespoke ware and everywhere required — young flesh. All of it proscribed and therefore even more desired and sought-after.

The Volunteers and Sinn Fein had their *Ard Fheis* as always in some town near the border. Speaker after speaker extolling passionately their desire for a United Ireland and an equal and all-inclusive society. The private screening in a side room later that evening of Jessie's newest flick *'Three men and a dirty little lady'* certainly was not that. None of the up and coming young, seriously fervent, female things were invited. Not to that and most certainly not to the 'reward' party afterwards.

South Armagh. Bandit country. The men and by now the very few women of the Ulster Defence Regiment and of course the RUC are locked into their base for months on end, on tour with whatever Army regiment is resident. Not much to do after a long day spent staring out of a Sanger's bomb proof window or on return from the unmitigated terror of patrolling the never-ending hedgerows and twisting lanes of the border. Fraternising is not permitted, can't have the Green Finches and the women officers of the RUC seen as objects to salve the men's needs. Any consorting with the opposite sex will have you demobbed soon as like.

Therefore, many a slimeball of a misogynist would rent and play one of Jessie's more famous works in the mess after dinner and would encourage the men present to get their toggers out in an effort to embarrass the young women and send them running, humiliated and pursued by mocking laughter to their beds.

So, it went on. Jessie built on his success, amassing contacts without fear or favour on both sides of the divide and in doing so stockpiling secrets on those who used his services, secrets that would translate into influence when he would come to need it.

An IRA training camp here, girls sneaked into the barracks there. Police retirement dinners, escorts at stag functions. Shoots at the Manor and private gentlemen's clubs for the well-to-do and massage parlours with or without happy endings for Joe public. Orange or Green, Jessie didn't care and with his rise in station came a desire to uncover his roots.

The Sailor's Rest

I'd been here before, cold, wet and wobbly and barely the strength to stand. The rain had soaked me to the skin and the gusts blowing and swirling through the square had chilled me to the bone as I tried to summon the courage to go in. What the fuck was I doing?

Then as if something else controlled me, I started across the now familiar cobbles though the double doors and without looking at the far corner made my way to the bar and climbed exhausted and shivering onto my old faithful stool.

'What'll you have?' Jesus, he spoke to me. I relished in my promotion, in my change of grade to regular status. I had finally become worthy of his attention.

'Just a glass of water, please,' I murmured trying to hunker down into my borrowed hoody.

'Don't sell water,' such distain, and I realised I'd immediately fallen in his estimation, crushed after my brief sojourn on the higher plane of pub existence.

'No problem,' I said, 'a free glass will do.' My God, comebacks at the once scary staff, what giving yourself over to your own self-destructive impulses can do for you.

He grabbed a glass and once sure I was watching, kept his fingers in it as he filled it from the tap before slapping it down in front of me. 'You look like shite!' he offered, before turning away back to his Racing Post.

I just held the drink in my hand and let my fever hot wrist

rest against the cool glass. As the condensation soaked slowly through my dressing, I ventured a glance around.

Jessie was sitting with his feet up on a chair smoking a cigarette and reading his little black book. The blobby brothers were positioned, one each side of the booth staring ahead, the uglier of them nonchalantly picking his nose, probably trying to catch a thought or two in the vast empty spaces of their skulls. A fierce shiver ran up my spine, down my arms and turned into a violent shake that had me set the glass down before I dropped it and drew all that unwanted attention to myself.

The flesh remembers.

I would have to wait until they left him unguarded again, however long that would be. Hoping for some sort of distraction, I looked along the bar in case that same kind patron had left his copy of the Sun behind but no go. I was stuck with my thoughts and they didn't cheer me.

'So, it's come to this. The final act. The denouement,' Karine said softly into my mind.

'It's no such thing. He'll give me something this time, I know it,' I replied, feverishly glad to hear her voice.

'Oh! Sher. You know you don't believe in this stuff, so stop tormenting yourself with this delusion you're holding on to. You know that you'll not end up happily ever spiritually-after with us. You know that any promised hereafter is here-never. All you will achieve is an ending, a numbness, a nothing,' she said, and I could almost hear the tears running down her cheeks.

'I… I have nothing anyway,' I replied. 'I have an empty home echoing with ghostly voices and laughter, and of course a baby crying. When I'm there — little enough anyway as I've sort of moved into the hospital — I sit and stare at the wall and cry.'

'You also know that I would want you to live and to find

some sort of happiness,' she offered. 'There's time for you yet, to start again, to find some peace, to find someone else.'

'Ha! You would have had me killed to save our child!' and I couldn't help the bitterness spilling into my voice.

The barman glanced over at my mumbling to myself and the tears running down my cheeks and sniffed loudly in disgust. Permanently relegated from the heights of regular status no doubt.

'You're wrong Sher. In those few seconds I was swamped with huge feelings and a thousand thoughts. I struggled with my duty, as did you, but I grabbed on to the only thing I was sure of. You loved me! Me! You loved me. How could that not be the most important thing in my life?

I don't know what showed on my face, I'm frightened to think that I might have given you the wrong impression. I was scared and panicking. I don't know if what you said was out of love or because you felt you had to, but I wasn't going to let him take you from me. As much as I also loved our child, I had decided to let her go if necessary.'

'You're only saying this now to try and make me feel better,' I said.

'Well. In reality, you're only saying this now to make yourself feel better,' and there was such a familiar smile in her voice that it made my heart ache.

'Don't do it Sher. Please,' her soft pleading nearly unmanned me.

'I have to, more, I want to,' I replied.

'McCracken handed you this 'tip' and you saw what would happen. You knew you didn't have it in you to end things for yourself and you grabbed on to that like the loaded revolver it was. All you need now is for that primped and preened porpoise penis to pull the trigger for you. Don't. I beg you, please!'

'Thank you, my love. I know that you're the part of me that is frightened and is trying to talk me out of this, but I can pretend for a little while further that you're here with me, it shouldn't take long,'

I felt a new energy fill me, coruscating down through my body. 'I will have my say with that fucker,' and then the veil lifted. Oh! I'd known from the start. From the time I first walked in here impelled by the Chief Inspector of turds' handy information. I just hadn't allowed myself to see it.

Then as if the Gods in their heavens actually existed and were laughing as they shifted our stinking little corpuscles around at their unknowable whim, the fat boys moved.

As Porker and Porkier left through the door, I heaved myself off my old faithful stool and weaved among the few tables towards Jessie. He looked up from his notebook in surprise at me approaching and said, 'Whatever it is, fuck off son. I'm not in the mood.' Then as I took another step forward, I pulled down my hood. He started from his seat, drawing his feet down from the chair and leaping up just as my outstretched hand hit him in the sternum with all the force I could muster.

'Sit the fuck down! You little oily prick!' I said, doing my best impression of a snarl. Gods below who was this new me! He looked around him for his two best buddies and for a moment a touch of fear showed in his eyes. It was like manna to the famished Israelites. It flushed through me like a good orgasm and set off sparks in my brain.

'You've had your fat-fuck goons hurt me and embarrass me and you've played your little games with my hand, with your tiny little hammer and chisel and thought yourself a God. You've frightened me like all the people you distain, coming to you for favours like some cheap-rate, half-price, dick-head Godfather. You've held me in contempt for no reason other than I wanted to ask you a question!' By this time, I was spitting into his face, leaning over the table from a distance of ten inches or so.

'My wife's name was Karine! Some fat wobbly fuck killed her in our kitchen in front of me and our baby daughter. She was the most important thing in my life and the only thing of beauty and grace in this much-fucked, half-blown-to shite, turd-heap of a country by a country mile. She was the mother of my child, the light of my life and SHE. WAS. YOUR. SISTER!' My voice broke at the end as I was shouting so loudly and every sad drunken bugger in the place paused in the act of slowly killing themselves to listen.

In the silence, the creak of the doors ushered in the shorn mammoths and they looked very worried indeed as they caught their boss's eye. I on the other hand felt no worry at all as I slumped down on the chair recently blessed with Jessie's polished pimp shoes.

'Karine. Big sis. Fuck me!' and he held up his hand to stop the stampede which sort of bumbled to a stop a few feet away. 'I've heard nothing about her in months. Sister Concetta used to keep track of her comings and goings for me, but I haven't seen hide nor habit of her in donkey's.'

He drew to a halt, looked up at the pillars of Hercules with a snide look in his eye and said, 'Well, that's all the niceties dealt with and brother-in-law or not a man's word is his bond,' and he got to his feet and pointed at me. Once again, I felt the pincers closing on my shoulders and he led the way, marching through the bar to the door leading to the back room. I was pulled along feet dangling and dragging on the slabs, head swinging around trying to catch the eye of any punter with a pulse and a modicum of moral fibre, but there was obviously much more interesting, life enhancing things going on in their glasses, and I was ignored.

The back room looked like it did before and that didn't please me in any way. However, I was pushed down into the seat by the table without the comforting straps tied to me this time. Jessie leaned, nonchalantly, against the closed door and took out a cigarette and lit it.

'These things have to be done. There's no getting away from it. A man means what he says, or he is rightfully ignored as a mendacious cunt. Order must be maintained, respect restored,' he said, blowing smoke up into the air. 'I'd be lying if I said this was going hurt me more than you.' The twins tried hard to laugh at this witticism like all good sycophants should but could manage no more than a slight twist of the lips. He ignored them.

'I'd also be lying if I said that I take no pleasure in this. It gives me a cucumber hard-on just thinking about it,' he said, grinding out his cigarette butt on the doorframe and letting it fall to the floor.

'Whose turn is it this time.'

'Mine Boss,' came the growl from one of the papa bears.

'Fuck!' from the other, 'I really wanted him, that little prick's been getting on my nerves since we had to slap him that time.'

'Tough shit!' came the gruff reply. 'You got that skank with the bleached hair last month and I wanted her.'

'If I'd known we could have done a swap. She was no fun anyway,' growled Papa Bear Two a bit miserably.

'Boys. Boys. If you've finished your little entertaining banter, let's get on.' Jessie was almost purring now that everything was back as it should be. 'Rarebit, he's all yours but wait a for an hour or so until things get quieter. Wolfgang you're with me, I've an urgent need to feed. Drop me off and come back to help him with the necessary. All right! Good! Let's get to fuck.' With that he opened the door behind him, and a very disappointed looking Papa Bear Two and Jessie left me alone with Papa Bear One.

Being locked in a dingy room with a thirty stone psycho-gorilla murmuring over and over again, incessantly for an hour or more, 'Gonna smash your bones, Gonna drink your blood, Gonna crush your head. Gonna smash your bones, Gonna drink your blood, Gonna crush your head.' While staring at you with tiny little evil eyes wasn't how I'd wished to spend my final moments on this good green earth, but you get what you get.

It was a genuine relief when the noise stopped, and the piggy little ears pricked up at some sound I couldn't hear. Then he bounded across the room and grabbed me around the neck with one meaty, smelly arm and hauled me out of the chair while he opened the door and dragged me, kicking and twisting and shouting for help, through to the little cobbled bit I'd seen before at the back of the pub.

He threw me to the ground, into the wet and the muck, into a space between the crates and the bottles and the empty steel casks and I cracked the back of my head off the cobbles. A little glazed, I looked up at him launch himself into the air in what wrestling afficionados would know as a Diving Elbow drop. His body would land on mine with his elbow leading causing his whole weight to crush my throat.

I was a little amazed at my detachment and watched him soar into the air quite gracefully for a pug-ugly boar and turned inwardly to smile at Karine as I waited for the pain to cease forever.

The flesh remembers; but it also wants to live.

While I was gazing with awe, detached in a way I couldn't understand and laughing somewhere inside my head with Karine at the thought of actual flying pig, my hand was groping in a desperate attempt by my sub-conscious to realise some means, even at that last moment, to survive. I was startled to find myself grasping a smooth round object and pulling it in towards my side just as the heavy fat fucker landed.

There was a meaty sort of slappy sucky noise followed immediately by a loud crack as his elbow missed me and hit the cobbles by my head. Then his weight hit me, and all my breath left me, as the ribs on my right side broke.

My chest was in agony, I was gasping for air, but my lungs wouldn't inflate, and he started to buck and squirm, almost as if he were trying to have sex with me. The strange, passionate sounding moaning didn't help and then as his weight kept me from breathing and blackness claimed me, I could swear I could feel the wetness of his spend on my thigh.

I awoke in the rain. I took a deep breath and was awarded with a stabbing agony. I lay still for a minute, breathing as shallowly as I could, taking stock. I was on my back with a stream running around me to enter the drain in the centre of the space, my head parting the waters like a bridge pylon in a river. In the light from the streetlamp, I could see a massive bulk of meat collapsed at the door into the pub. A huge river of red had flowed from a massive wound in its side and the bloody remains of a Veuve Clicquot champagne bottle was grasped in its hairy paw.

I forced myself to turn over and after the dizziness abated a little and I stopped wanting to die with the pain, I got to my knees. Blood was all over me from the waist down but as far as I could tell none of it was mine.

I was alive and I didn't know how I felt about that. I'd killed a man, another living, breathing human being, a scumbag it is true but still, a life ended by my hand. I was swamped with guilt and pain and shaky with adrenaline overload, so I threw up over his feet.

The Incinerator

Charlie hated this bit, though thankfully he had only had to do it on three other occasions, but a job's a job and he was grateful for it, even though he knew that this sort of job was one that you never left, or ever quit from. A sanctioned retirement was the best anyone could ask for — if that didn't turn out to be a bullet in the head and a wet grave.

It was his hope that he could just skim enough to put a bit aside, enough aside for a house of his own. A time that would see him and Margaret living in their own little cottage by the sea down Millisle way, or any of the other seaside villages on the Ards peninsula.

Fuck! This little one looked about his grandson's age — Mildred's boy, Ash — just the image of him as well. Still best get this done and get home.

He called at his friend Alan's house on the way and picked up the key to the City Incinerator out on Dargan Road. Thankfully, he didn't have to sit around waiting for the place to close up as he had before. Not stuck twiddling his thumbs parked by the side of the road with a thing in the boot, just terrified that the RUC would come by and decide to hassle him and take a look.

He let himself in through the gates and drove over to the loading bay for No.2 furnace. Having entered through the sallyport, he raised the corrugated metal door, cringing at the creaks and the loud metallic squeaks and squeals as it shuddered in its ungreased track. Finally, it was up, and he drove his car in and let the door down again to screen him from the road.

He walked the short distance to the heaped pile of rubbish and effluent waiting, stinking, and giving off steam from the decaying organic matter buried amongst it, to be shovelled into the great maw of the furnace by the stained yellow bulldozer sitting to one side.

Charlie approached the pile, wary of the rats that liked it so much, looking for large sheets of plastic to wrap the 'evidence' in, along with some rope to secure things.

Having found some excellent pieces, he returned to his car and popped the boot. Christ! The little body curled up there nearly had him choking again. Girding his loins, he reached in and picked the child up, still warm. He was always amazed at how long they stayed warm for, how slowly the bodies lost their heat.

He pushed at the plastic with his feet and rearranged it to give himself a flat place to lay the boy down. As he did so the boy groaned, and he nearly shit himself and dropped him. Can't be, he thought, and the boy groaned again. What the fuck was he going to do now?

He held his head in his hands for a moment and then wandered over to the rubbish pile to find a large piece of wood with some nails in it. Returning and standing straddled over the boy, he raised the plank above his head and stopped. He couldn't do this. He couldn't smash the little tyke's head in. How could he live with himself, face Margaret and Mildred again? He might be a nasty type of bastard sometimes, but he wasn't a child killer. Fuck that.

But what to do? He couldn't take the boy home, that would raise far too many questions he couldn't even begin to answer.

He could just drop him at the hospital or at the door to the church, they'd see him right. But what if the boy talked? It would come back to bite Charlie in a very big way, right in the middle of his skull way.

There was only one place he could think off that might fit and if she was up for it, he might even get a bit off, or heaven forbid if he was lucky, his whole slate wiped clean. Selling the child was a bit down there but he wasn't an angel was he.

He loaded the kid in the back of the car and worked his way out of the complex and down the road into the city and to the establishment in Customs House Square, so pleased with himself and his answer to his problem that he actually laughed.

Jessie

Where do we begin? What do we define ourselves as? We start to answer these questions when we understand our history, our connections to the past through generations of ancestors. Am I British or Irish is a favourite one for these times? Am I Orange or Green or some grey flavour steeped in self-denial, arguing against my nature until the ballot box beckons?

Jessie considered his nature understood but now, with his business blossoming along with its inherent ability to fast track his path to influence, he desired to know of his beginnings.

In those memories of his childhood, that he dared to look at, nothing remained to guide him but a name. He knew his sister and he felt that she had stood as his protector, though not why. He knew her name was Karine. Of his parents, nothing.

His recollections of life before Madam's were vague and useless and any help she and the girls may have been was lost, lost along with the building he had spent so many painful years in. Lost because he had sent them burning and howling to their crisp black, graves.

Karine, his big sister, what had happened to her? A child alone but not snatched by the opportunistic, would undoubtedly fall into the hands of the state or the Catholic church. Access to the state information was bound to be slow and by the book, so time to use a little of that influence he'd garnered.

He pressed a particular priest he'd been hearing about, massaging not squeezing, and within a week a letter arrived requesting him to meet at a parochial house in the west of the city, one of those old three storey Victorian things, all cold stone and damp, with a tiny overgrown garden at the front surrounded by a mildewed brick wall topped with rusty black iron railings.

He was shown into the parlour after stamping the slush from his feet on the welcome mat by the door. It was unused and chilly, musty with mould and old cigarette smoke and in great need of new paint. The priest sat at a faded wooden desk and invited him to take the hard wooden seat opposite. Tea was delivered by an ancient housekeeper and provided in small porcelain cups and poured from a big old iron teapot. Accompanying the tea were a few McVitie's digestive biscuits looking lonely and forlorn on a large unmatching plate, but he declined them when offered.

The priest took a while getting started but finally with a few coughs he managed, 'I don't believe I'm guilty of the things you wrote about me and I categorically deny any and all suggestions that you made concerning my time at St. Malachy's.'

'Father,' said Jessie, gently, pushing his cup towards the centre of the table and crossing his legs, 'I don't care and I'm not here to judge. I just want information. Did you find out anything about her?'

'Ahem! Right. Well. As long as it's understood that there is nothing to judge, I could see my way to providing something to help you.' The priest paused and closed his eyes for a few moments, bringing his hands together and lacing his fingers, perhaps in an effort to remember, perhaps in supplication.

'There was only one girl of that name ever taken into the system and she was placed into the care of the sisters at St. Glaphyra's near Ardglass, Co. Down.' He now opened his eyes and looked at Jessie, unclasping his hands and holding them out palm up, 'However, most unfortunately, she was a wilful child,

175

always causing trouble and offence. Constantly being punished, as kindly as possible you understand, in a bid to remove whatsoever demons drove her. In the end we failed. The church failed her, and she escaped from our care some years later.'

'So, you don't know her whereabouts or what happened to her afterwards,' Jessie said, uncrossing his legs and leaning into the priest's space. He let a little of his frustration leak into anger and threat, 'Have I come all this way to have you waste my time, Father?'

'Sweet Mother of Jesus! No,' the priest said quickly, leaning back and holding his hands up in the air. 'She was enrolled in Our Lady of Mercy's school a few months later and we kept an eye on her comings and goings — only in the casual sense, you understand — a conversation here, a little chat there. It was decided to leave her as she was, as forcing her back into the home might prove difficult and frankly, a waste of time.

She lived in the town until she was sixteen, in a little cottage by the harbour, quietly and unobtrusively, with an old fisherman — not a relation as we understand it — and as far as we can tell moved to Belfast after he was lost at sea. I have a colleague currently looking for any further news of her.'

'Good. That's something anyway. Perhaps enough. We'll have to see,' and Jessie got up to leave, buttoning his overcoat.

'Ahem! Right. Well. Just a minute, I'd like to introduce you to my colleague who will liaise with you from now on, should we find out anything more.' The Father got up and came back a few seconds later leading a nun. Jesus! What a nun.

Jessie didn't actually believe that women could get that big, how did they ever find a wimple and habit for her, must have come from Giants 'R' Us, or more probably from the circus. She followed the priest into the room to stand towering over Jessie, saying not a word.

'This is Sister Concetta-Patricia, Jessie. This is Jessie, Sister. Concetta is actually an alumnus of your sister, as she was at St. Glaphyra's too, though a year or so later I believe. Funnily enough she came to me once I started making inquiries. Apparently, she has a great interest in the girls who passed through our hands at the home, and intends to contact them all, in an effort to create an old girl's association or some such.'

Jessie said his goodbyes and leaving the old house, walked along the wet street still thinking about the meeting with the priest and the very large nun and happy, in a way, that Karine was out there somewhere, maybe a stone's throw away living her life, content. So involved with those thoughts, was he, and the possibility of a reconnection with his sister in the near future, that he failed to notice the motorcycle slowly tracking him a few metres behind.

As he turned the corner back to his car, the motorcycle accelerated past him in a cloud of noise and two-stroke exhaust smoke. It was a few seconds before he noticed the blood running down the inside of his coat and dripping on to his feet and a few more before he collapsed at his car, key in his hand.

Jessie woke in hospital, bandages around his chest and tubes in his arms. All sorts of beeps coming from the drip machine and monitors by his head. He was in a two-bed bay in the ward but could see nobody in the bed alongside, however, he could just make out a shape sitting in the chair in the corner.

'What the fuck happened?' he slurred.

'Don't fuss yourself, son, I'll get a nurse,' the shape said, getting up and leaving for a minute.

A nurse bustled in, all blue and white uniform and perkiness. She brightly said hello and asked if he was OK, then tucked him in a little and went and picked up the charts at the end of the bed. While scribbling something, she told him that he'd been shot in the chest and had undergone emergency surgery, which he'd come through, fine and dandy, and that he'd be back on his feet in no time. The doctor and consultant would fill in the details, if he required any further information, during morning rounds.

She left and the shape came back, now in much better focus. A large man in a crumpled grey suit, short spikey hair and a bad mood, 'Chief Inspector John-Henry McCracken,' he introduced himself, standing where the nurse had stood. 'Just called in on the off chance that you were *compos mentis*, and to see if you could enlighten me?'

'Enlighten you? Chief Inspector. What do you mean?' Jessie said, trying to push himself up on the bed to a more comfortable position.

McCracken sighed and moved to lean over him, pointing one large forefinger in an aggressive manner, 'Listen son, I don't like people getting shot on my patch even if they are toe-rags, unless I do the shooting of course,' he gave a little dry laugh. 'As far as I can tell you're not one of the boyos nor one of the prod fuck-heads from over the fence, so I'm going to assume that this,' his finger moved to encompass the large dressings wrapped around Jessie, 'was a case of mistaken identity,' how does that sound to you?

Jessie gave up trying to adjust his position and slumped down where he was, 'Mistaken identity, must have been, who would want to shoot me, for Christ's sake?' he replied.

'Mmm, who indeed?' McCracken said, turning for the door, 'You take care of yourself.' He took two steps, 'I'll be watching now that I know you. Cheerio now!' he threw over his shoulder as he left.

Jessie was worried, getting shot can do that to a fella. How had he pissed off someone enough to want to shoot him? He did push a little now and again but felt sure that he'd have had a warning before the big one. Eventually he'd worried at it enough and fell asleep.

A few days later, he was up and moving around and taking his lunch in the chair in the corner instead of on his bed. He looked up at a soft knock on the door frame and a smallish bald man, stocky and holding an unlit cigar, walked in and sat on the end of the bed facing him and stared into his eyes.

Paralysing fear swept through Jessie as he recognised him, and his bladder let go to allow urine to dribble down his thighs and groin unto the chair beneath him. The flesh remembers.

'Hello Jessie,' the man had a recollected huskiness to his voice that chilled Jessie to the bone. 'Don't know if you remember me, it's been a few years?' he said. 'Guess how surprised I was, when I realised that it was you I needed to see?'

Jessie tried his best to regain some control, forcing himself to break the ice gripping his mind and biting back at the emotions crowding him. He struggled to stamp down on the fear and swallowing hard and gripping his tray, 'No, can't say that I do,' was all that he could manage in response.

'Well, it's of no consequence,' the man stared for a moment longer and then smiled, took a box of matches from his pocket and pointed at Jessie with them. 'You know, you've been getting a bit ambitious Jessie, my boy. A man like me in the business for a long time, a man like me, who *is* the business in this country in fact, cannot allow competition to flourish. I'm sure you understand that.'

Jessie nodded tentatively, trying not to squirm in his sodden pyjamas, all too aware that the smell of his discharge must be reaching this man and demonstrating his fear.

'Good. Glad to know that you're up to speed. Oh! And just so you know,' the man paused, took out a match and lit his cigar, huffing and puffing and taking his time to get it going smoothly. 'The shooter missed, but he's very, very, very, sorry and assures me that he won't miss again if we just give him another chance,' he drew deeply on his cigar. 'Let's not give him one,' he said, and blew a cloud of smoke at Jessie, then stood to loom over him, adding, 'Eh! That's a good boy,' and poked his finger in Jessie's wound. 'Bye now.'

He walked out smiling to himself to the sound of Jessie screaming in pain.

The next week after being discharged, Jessie was holed up in his apartment with its ultra-sparse shiny décor, treading the same wall to window circuit that he'd been doing for hours while he thought about his life and his future. Should he walk away, craven, crushed, and beaten. Should he allow his past, and that fucking bald-headed, cigar smoking cunt to take what he had built, and had suffered so to build. No. No fucking way! Was his answer.

He would need to protect himself and to that end he needed some people he could trust around him. Seeing that turd had brought back hideous memories, but he wasn't a child any more, he didn't need to fear any more, he wasn't alone any more. He had friends, and people who owed him their influence, who owed him favours, people he owned.

A rising anger bloomed in his heart, a voracious rage to blow away the fear. How dare that fucker and the measures of the past keep him afraid, how dare that man wake that horror, take away his manhood and push him back into a little boy's trembling terror. It was time to put those memories and events away for ever, and to do that, he would put those men away forever.

If there was a god of vengeance he was listening, and he smiled on Jessie and blessed him.

Less than a week after his epiphany, he was summoned to a meeting with the West Belfast commander of the IRA to discuss the presence of, and hopefully to collect, certain goods included in a shipment of arms and explosives from South Africa.

As usual he waited alone and was picked up at an agreed location and taken with a hood over his head. Very often, as indeed now, he recognised the meeting site, but he knew the purpose of the pickup was more about the timescale than the place. Difficult to arrange any betrayal in that short piece of time.

After the usual driving around aimlessly to check for any followers, he was led into a garage near Casement Park and along a corridor created by knocking holes in the whole row of garages, he passed a pair of very strange looking individuals, over-large bulky types wearing battledress fatigues, tied to old wooden chairs bolted to the concrete in the middle of the floor.

Curious but sensitive to his situation he asked nothing of his guide, who eventually led him to a small windowless, concrete room that smelled of engine oil and grease and old sweat. Four people were waiting for him, three hidden behind balaclavas and carrying their pistols at the ready and standing, spread out, behind a fourth sitting behind a small desk.

Assuming the empty seat was for him, Jessie sat down and with a show of confidence he certainly didn't feel, lent forward and took a cigarette from the packet on the desk. He glanced at each of the standing men in turn and was struck by how silly they all looked, with their mixed green jackets and unmatched firearms. He would have laughed if his situation wasn't so fraught.

He was examined as he did so, by a gruff sort, maybe a son of the land, weather beaten and a little worn down. No greeting, no chitchat, piercing blue eyes in red-veined orbs, and a barely contained sense of menace, 'I've told you before, we are not your personal delivery service. This ends now. The only question is how it ends,' said the man on the other side of the desk, as he looked meaningfully around at the armed volunteers.

'Mr McKee, I've the greatest respect and admiration for you and yours and I won't presume on you again. It was just a matter of convenience. However, while you were struggling with those Arab boys and that madman in Libya and getting nowhere fas…'

'Watch it, you cheeky cunt,' interrupted one of the men at the rear.

'I mean no disrespect Martin,' Jessie said looking up at the volunteer standing directly behind the man at the desk, 'but it was my man in Cape Town that was able to uncover that little cache as a by-product of sourcing my stuff. There are things in there that will prove to be useful to you no doubt. Think on this, it was he who brokered the whole thing, collected and shipped on time, but more importantly delivered, secure and safe.'

He paused and lit his cigarette, absurdly pleased that his hand wasn't shaking. 'I know how you see me. I am under no illusion, I am at worst, a creep and flesh-pedlar and at best a tolerated source of necessary entertainment, but I think you must agree that I have been more than useful to you on this one. To put it plain, it's me you have to thank for this little lot,' and he bravely blew his smoke upwards into the air while he swept his hands around trying to encompass the goods, wherever they were.

The man opposite thought for a moment, and simply said, 'Granted. Now fuck off before I remember that I hate you.'

Jessie kept his seat, rolled the dice and poked the Kodiak

bear, 'Well, I was feeling that a little quid pro quo might be in order.'

'Jesus! You've got some fucking neck on you boy, I'll give you that,' the man replied. He was silent for a few seconds eyes locked on to Jessie, and then he waved the gunmen away and waited until they were alone. 'Tell me. What shite are you in this time or, more likely, what shite do you want to put me in this time?'

As they were walking out a little later, Jessie pushed his luck, 'Strange uniforms for those Brits to be wearing,' he nodded ahead to where the two men were tied-up.

'Not Brits, just two big dumb farm boys from the Transvaal, deserted the SAFD it seems and stowed away to have some fun fighting here, or so they say. It's a fucking joke. Who do these people think we are? A social club? Coming here at a drop of a hat without an invite. I mean, no fucker in their right mind would think that was going to work, fucking idiots.'

'Are they for the…' Jessie made a cutting motion across his neck.

'Don't know what else we can do with them, the daft fuckwits, they're for the deep dark right enough.'

'I don't suppose I could have them — my responsibility?' Jessie ventured.

'Fuck me! Like I said, you've some neck on you, so, on your neck be it. Take the cunts with you then. And Jessie,' he paused, stopped Jessie with a hand to his shoulder and half turned to face him staring once more into his eyes, and then with enough menace in his voice to give Jessie palpitations, said, 'No more fuck ups of any sort. Hear me, boy?'

Halloween. The smell of low explosive gunpowder hung in the

misty air over the damp streets. Fireworks were still illegal in our little corner of the UK/Ireland but that didn't stop their use. As with anything banned, the price simply went up as the desirability of doing something enjoyable but prohibited, with little chance of reproach, attracted people.

The man Cullen was leaving a shebeen he owned in the Ardoyne, replete with whiskey and cash from the whores who turned up to pay their dues as usual every Thursday night. He had enjoyed himself tonight and he'd enjoy himself more when he got home to that whiny bitch of a wife, wake her up though it was past midnight and make her work for her living. He had even enjoyed slapping Kirsty around for holding back, not that she had, but lessons needed be reinforced where money and whores were concerned.

Caught short on his way to his car, he turned into an alley and stopped for a piss against the wall and was thinking that things in these bad, black times shone golden for him, when he noticed the shadows. He looked up to find two men in front of him and turned his head to find two behind.

He wasn't concerned yet, his hooks were all in place. 'Look fellas. Listen. I pay my way and I'm up with my contributions, are you sure you've got the right man,' he said to the shadow in front him.

'Take him,' said a voice. And he was grabbed and dragged, protesting the whole time that he was the wrong man, to the alley entrance and bundled into a waiting car.

People in the neighbourhood were a little surprised. They would pass each other in the street, 'I never thought that of him,' or meet on the corner, 'Jesus you just don't know do you.' Even in the hairdressers, 'I know he was a flesh-sucking creep but that.'

Touts — informers — are the most hated in such places, and for them the most severe punishment is kept especially in reserve. The man Cullen was found an hour or so later in a pub car park on the Andersonstown Road, a bullet hole in each kneecap and then some minutes later, according to the autopsy, a bullet in each elbow. He was allowed to squirm in agony for another few minutes before his tongue was cut out and a final bullet in the back of his head ended his pain.

The man Cullen was a smallish man, thick-set, bald-headed and a cigar smoker. The man Cullen was taken in settlement of a debt, and the first of six on Jessie's road to vengeance.

Jessie relaxed and let himself laugh. God that was so easy. A small pressure and a bit of a bang, a hideous splat and spray, and one fucker less to trouble the youth of the world.

He had left the Casement with the two overlarge men in their desert scrubland fatigues and they were dropped off at Queens Street where had left his car. He was just about able to squeeze them into his Corina GT, and with high hopes in his heart he drove to an old pub he was thinking of buying and settled them down with a pint or two each.

Windhoek, in Namibia, South West Africa was home, not the Transvaal nor any other province of South Africa. Wolfgang and Rar something that Jessie immediately shortened to Rarebit, were indeed farm boys from the veld, but that was a long time ago.

Convergent evolution it is called in nature, but perhaps just a closed gene pool Jessie thought, that produced two such individuals that looked so alike. Three hundred pounds of cruel Afrikaans beef brought up on a Plaas miles from each other. Running away from home and the attentions of their respective local police forces, they joined the SAFD (South African

Defence Force) at sixteen and developed a serious taste for torturing the Kaffirs. A taste that immediately bonded them and one they enjoyed sharing when running down the PLAN (People's Liberation Army of Namibia) at home or in Zambia or burning the FAPLA (People's Armed Forces of Liberation of Angola) out of villages in Angola. The boytjies even had a joyous evening with a Cuban Advisor, caught at a PLAN camp in Namibia. They put him in the camp's communal cooking pot with plenty of water and boiled him. Even when the skin and meat started to fall from his bones, he continued to live and to scream.

Peace talks worried them, P. W. Botha's plan for ending apartheid and the rumour that Mandela was soon to be released made them much more so. In their cups they talked long into the night about what to do. They needed a conflict — not a war — a nice juicy messed up conflict with no leash and no rules, where they could continue to have a good time and get paid for it.

They often topped up their wages with extra-curricular work. They worked as bouncers and bodyguards for the scum whose rackets often placed them at risk, people smarter than them who paid well. Then one of these little side deals, running protection for a quartermaster selling off some old FAPLA mines and AK47s, introduced them to Northern Ireland, the six counties, the north of Ireland and our, to them, pleasing lack of Kaffirs.

Their dream was born. This was their way out. Nobody was going to try and bring them back from this Ireland place for a few bruised Kaffirs — not worth the effort. They read what they could find on the Provisionals and decided that they would be a good fit, they could transform their military expertise into a nice plum position with these white freedom fighters far from any possible future peace and reconciliation tribunals.

So it was, that they found themselves tucked in with the crates on a tramp steamer, on its way to Dundalk in the Irish Republic and the incredulity of the RA men unloading it in the dead of night.

The man Cullen's funeral gave Jessie two faces, and once he'd shaken off the shock and fear triggered by seeing them again, and by force of will replacing it with a cold burning rage, he set out to mix with the mourners. A bit of charm and chat at the wake gave him two names and general addresses. The rest was simple.

This time he borrowed from his friends — The Shankill Butchers — whose modus operandi was to ride with an unsuspecting taxi driver. Once the bogus passengers had established the driver's religion with certainty, a .22 to the back of the head sealed the deal.

Terror abounded at the thought that any innocent could be picked on. A brilliant tactical move or just dumb, sectarian murderous luck, we'll let posterity decide. Taxi drivers became much more cautious and suspicious, understandably so, but Jessie had an easy answer.

He used one of his many eager actresses and went to a certain pub, kept his head down and let her drink herself into oblivion and paid a handsome contribution to the cause when the boyos came round with their baskets. He then staggered with her to the taxi office at a time his target was at work and again the vengeance god was watching and blessed him. His boy was in the queue waiting for a fare, and by judicious pausing to let the woman get her breath or throw up, he hit the head of the queue at just the right time. A man and a woman on a date, both seemingly drunk, her out of it, were unlikely assassins.

Jessie bundled her into the back seat and climbed in after her.

He gave the cabbie an address in the west of the city that was immediately accepted without comment and pretended to fall asleep like the woman beside him.

After twenty minutes or so, Jessie slowly took the .22 he had been lent from his pocket as he lay against the taxi window and wondered how many notches were on its handle, how many lives this weapon had ended already. He also wondered if he'd have the balls to do it now that the moment was approaching.

About half a mile short of his supposed destination on the Bell Steel Road he sat forward and asked the taxi driver to pull over, so that his date and he could sober up a bit with a walk in the cold night air. This wasn't a problem and as the taxi pulled to the curb on a mostly deserted bit of the street, Jessie said to the driver, 'You'll rape no more kids, you cunt,' put the gun to the back of his head and pulled the trigger.

The twins picked them up a few seconds later and Jessie sat in the back seat and laughed. Just a small pressure and a bit of a bang. It was easy.

Early December and the crippling affliction that was Christmas consumerism was rife in the shops and markets of Belfast as it was all over the world. The twins with their natty tribute to the season, lengths of red tinsel wrapped around their massive necks like flimsy scarves, pushed the man into the back of his own run-down, rusty van and climbed in with him.

He'd been doing a refurbishment job on some old semi-detached houses in the Old park area of the city, a fitter or joiner or such. They had waited across the road in the fading light for him to start loading his gear at the end of the day, and just came up behind him in the gloom when he was carrying his last load.

Jessie jumped into the passenger seat and was handed the

keys through the grill. They drove for a while to some waste ground on the Antrim Road, where Jessie asked his questions and the man eventually supplied the answers.

It was during this question-and-answer session that Jessie, in frustration, picked up a hammer from the man's tool bag and smashed it down on an exposed thumb. Pleased with the amount of pain this produced he rummaged further and choosing a slim chisel, proceeded to use it with great effect on the man's hands.

Long after the man had given all that he had to give, Jessie sat back, tossed the hammer and chisel into the bag with a loud metal clang and climbed out of the rear of the van. He lit a cigarette and walked to his car, leaned against the door and nodded to the twins who tossed a coin. Wolfgang won and he danced a little jig while ridiculing Rarebit, then at a stern glance from Jessie he climbed back into the van where he strangled their victim with a piece of electrical cable.

They left the van burning and Jessie flushed with a strange orgasmic like pleasure, dwelled on the noise and feeling of breaking bones, not with huge violence, but as gently as possible so that the dread of the next strike became all-encompassing. It was akin to a hammer and steel Chinese water torture he acknowledged, and sated in way like never before, he headed home to think on the names he'd been given. One of which had shocked him to his core.

Number four was a tad more difficult but not much more so, it was just a matter of surveillance and procuring access and then a works Christmas dinner offered a simple opportunity.

Jessie's sexuality was a matter of convenience to him, a thing to be switched on or off at his whim to lever profit or connection. Dressed in his finest he chatted up the local TV announcer, who was out with his colleagues, all boozed up at the latest fashionable, access restricted watering hole, and made it perfectly clear with his body language and inuendo, that he was up for anything.

He waited around until the dinner was over and sure enough the seat next to him at the bar was taken by the man, relatively famous in this small pond, who had ditched his compadres in search of a delicious, still discriminated against adventure. A few short drinks later and the plump blowhard was putty in his hands. Then a casual nudge in the right direction and he was invited to the man's chic new apartment, all stainless steel and bold windows with a glorious view over the city, for a nightcap.

After a performance well up with his best, he left his well satisfied lover asleep on his garish waterbed and in the dead hour of the early morning before dawn, went to the door intercom on the wall and buzzed in his twins.

The expensive noise reduction insulation was a boon and served to deaden the man's screams as Rarebit, laughing at his terror, cut off the victim's cock and rammed it into his anus. Then both the twins held him down while his life blood welled out of the wound to soak the cream silk sheets, it took nearly ten minutes and the creep was pleading and crying and promising the world the whole time.

Jessie sitting in the corner relaxing, in a height-of-fashion Swedish chair, enjoyed every moment.

All the New Year parties were long ago history and in the lengthy slog through a nasty cold January to the first wages of February a secondary school teacher waited.

One of the joys of living at that time in the mess that was Northern Ireland was the ability to make anything seem like a mistake by one side or the other.

Most fortunately, a man living alone in a particular part of town was bound to have a neighbour either next door or a few doors away with some connection to the security forces or to those 'elements of the crown's imperialistic regime' considered legitimate targets by the various republican factions — civilians mainly.

A car bomb destroys a family and the news reports that it was meant for a RUC officer living nearby — those sorts of easily made mistakes, not to be taken too seriously. After all, mistakes happen.

It takes time for people to wake up from their night's sleep, and say to themselves, 'What was that noise?' Decide that it sounds threatening, 'Next door maybe?' Then haul themselves from their beds, get dressed a little, puff themselves up to confront the threat and leave the safety of their houses for the unknown in the cold dark. Meanwhile.

In the dead of night three men in balaclavas with sledgehammers and pistols break in. The secondary school teacher wakes up and rushes to the top of his stairs where he sees the men and in panic he half turns to run away before the bullets enter his body.

The three men are gone in less than thirty seconds, before the neighbours are even properly awakened by the sound of the shots echoing amongst the houses.

The crime scene photos always seem so sad and forlorn. A middle-aged man lying on his landing with his feet jutting out over the top step, his thinning hair is a tousled mess. All he is wearing is his faded blue, dirty underwear and you can clearly see the huge holes in his side and back and half his face missing, jaw, bottom teeth and chin just visible a few feet away, never to be reached by the spread of the blood stain.

Jessie drank a celebratory whiskey in his new pub and his boys, now fully fused to him and loyal beyond a doubt, saluted him in turn. He was flushed and replete and revelled in the feeling of absolute power that was running through his veins. God what a rush.

The Courtyard Gallery was an up-and-coming *café du jour* for the lunch and afternoon tea crowd — if you were a certain age — and Jessie had decided that this place would suit his purposes admirably. He took a lot of care over his appearance and carried with him an exquisite bouquet of orchids; it was St. Valentine's Day, after all.

As he entered the café, he spotted his target, sitting alone at a table near the rear, thankfully with no easy egress. She was elegantly dressed in a cream two-piece overlaid with a silver-grey silk jacket and a scarlet cravat. The table was set for two and Jessie worried for a second that a companion might be away for a moment in the toilet, even though on the occasions he had spied on her she always ate alone.

He realised with relief that it was simply an artifice of the restaurant, perhaps to lessen the embarrassment some felt if noticed at a table for one. She had been served already and had a selection of finger sandwiches along with a variety of petit fours and tea in a service. He told the *maître d'* that he was expected and approached the table head on. When it was obvious that he was coming towards her, the woman raised her head, a look of quizzical alarm on her face.

Jessie said, 'Lady Maude, may I speak with you a moment?'

As Lady Maude looked at him in confusion, he offered the bouquet, 'These are for you.'

'Do I know you, young man?' she smiled as she replied, and squinting a little she picked up her glasses and put them on. 'Oh! These are lovely, thank you. But what on earth are they for?'

Jessie moved a little so that the light from the window could fall on his face, 'They're just to say thank you for all that you did for me.'

'What do you mean, did for you,' she said, then recognition bloomed, 'No. No. I don't think so. Get away from me before I have you thrown out. I have no wish to talk to you or even see your face. Get away!' she started to raise her voice but controlled herself as her neighbouring tea drinkers reacted.

Jessie was counting on just this, 'Of course I'll leave. I would never wish to cause you any further harm. I know I hurt you and embarrassed you, but I just wanted to say that I think of you all the time. That I'm grateful for the love and care you lavished on me and for the path that you put me on. I betrayed you, but thank you again, for making me what I have become,' he said, and then turned to slowly move away between the tables.

'Oh! Stop making a spectacle, Gerald. Sit down and have some tea.'

From this small beginning Jessie crafted a reconciliation. He met with Maude many times, and she hungry for attention, forgot the past, and embraced the new Gerald, presented as the embodiment of all that she had desired for him.

He waited patiently for the first mention of the Judge, never daring to bring him up. And his patience was finally rewarded when, at last, Maude said that she was sure that the Judge would like to meet him, to see how well he had turned out. Jessie demurely said that he was sure that the Judge would have nothing to do with him, despite his wishing to thank him in person.

It was that point in his life that changed things. That point when the Judge threw him out. That was the low point from which he slowly but surely dragged himself, putting to work the education lavished upon him and the effort and expense spent on him.

Jessie explained this with a tear in his eye and his hand holding Maude's, 'I wish I could let him know what a pivotal moment that was. My treatment at the hands of the Judge was exactly what I needed to turn my life around.' By the time he had finished Maude needed to wipe her own eye and this tipped the balance.

Maude unquestionably took that message home to the old man and by whatsoever means necessary wore him down and reported to Jessie that she and the Judge would meet him for lunch at a little bistro in Belfast, one o'clock Monday next. A place not too far from the courthouse but far enough away not to attract any of Francis's cronies.

Jessie was early and was sitting nervously when the Judge's close protection team came in and checked the premises. He was a bit concerned by one of them sitting at the table next along but need not have worried because the Old Beak, true to form and with his usual contempt, dismissed his protection to the car outside.

When they had all settled into their seats and Jessie had endured the Judge's scornful stare he broke the silence, 'Thank you for coming to meet me, Sir.'

'What is it you want, boy?' the Judge said with barely contained distain.

'Francis!' Maude hissed, 'Give the boy a chance,' nudging his arm.

'Thank you for coming, Sir,' said Jessie, starting again. 'I just wanted to thank you for all those things you did for me, taking me from that place and providing me with a home and a family, giving me opportunity and education. Of course, even in my earliest days you gave me such special attention.'

'What on earth are you blathering on about boy,' the Judge replied and then as two waiters approached with silver platters. 'We haven't even seen a menu yet, you fools!' The waiters stopped each side of the Judge and one bent down and whispered in his ear and then together they helped him up and led him to the kitchen at the rear.

'What the hell is going on?' said Maude, looking at Jessie. 'Francis, where are you going. Francis, Francis!'

Another man sat down in the seat recently vacated by the Judge, 'You will do exactly as I say, Mrs. McDermott, if you wish to see your man again.'

'What? What do you mean — see again,' the penny dropped for Maude when the man opened his jacket a little to let her see the holstered pistol. 'Oh! Oh no. Look don't hurt him. I'll do whatever you want. I will, I will, whatever you want.'

'Just sit here for at least ten minutes before you run out to the cavalry in the car outside. Ten minutes at least, our people will be watching,' the man said. 'In fact, why don't you order yourself some tea. 'You,' nodding at Jessie. 'You come with me.'

'Of course, Mr McKee, whatever you say.'

Judge Francis McDermott was tortured and after enduring unknown agonies was finally allowed to die some days later. A symbol of the British Imperialist rule in Ireland was removed, a coup of epic proportions and importance, never again to be accomplished by the Provisionals.

The Judge Francis McDermott was taken in settlement of a debt and was the last of six on Jessie's road, to vengeance.

The Bedroom

Six weeks since the baby had come home, and I was ready to throw it at the wall. Not that I dared say that, in any shape or form. I was doing my best to help but things were fraught and delicate.

She was breast feeding and while the baby slept between feeds, I would try and feed Karine. When Karine slept between feeds I would try and look after the baby. She was so tired she had fallen asleep with one breast still exposed and the baby on her chest. I couldn't help but look for a little longer and thought rather ungallantly, what a magnificent breast it was — sexist and inappropriate I know — but the flesh remembers. I decided to leave them undisturbed to sleep.

I put out some cut fruit for her breakfast, melon, black grapes and orange segments, cooked her a cheese and tomato omelette, added some toast and orange juice, and on the one hour forty-five-minute mark was setting the tray down on the bed and shaking her gently.

'Leave me the fuck alone, especially if you want to keep the use of your balls,' she was always so bright and happy at these times.

'Come on, wake up and eat something before the beast, I mean before the baby does,' I said softly.

She opened her eyes and as gently as she could lifted the baby up to me to put into her cot by the bed. This blessed thing had only been occupied for the last few days, but I was joyous about it. Prior to then I had to manage with just the edge of the bed while a tiny baby had more room than two adults used just to 'spread out'. As far as I could see it invariably rolled over until it could feel its mother anyway, leaving vast swathes of lovely mattress unpopulated.

I succeeded in setting baby down without waking her and as Karine sat up tucking away the goodies I placed the tray on her lap, ran around the other side and lay down and stretched languorously.

She started to eat and found herself ravenous, 'Sometimes you're not such a waste of space. I'd even go so far to say that on odd occasion you're sometimes positively useful,' she said generously.

'Thanks a bunch,' I said, then hopefully. 'How long is this going to go on for?'

'Until she wants to stop, I suppose. I'm not happy about bottle feeding and I'm certainly not going to put her in a cot in a room on her own to cry herself to sleep.'

Jesus! I thought, I'm already at the end of my tether, usurped by a few pounds of squalling meat, a feeling known to man since the beginning of baby kind. Oh! Well.

Karine finished her breakfast and I got up to take it away. I fully expected the baby to be awake and squealing when I got back but no, all was still quiet. I took full advantage and climbed straight back into bed. She snuggled up to me, 'Thanks for looking after me so well Sher.'

'No problem. Are you not going back to sleep?' I lifted my arm and pulled her closer.

'No point she'll be up in a minute. Tell me a story,' she said from under my shoulder.

'What. No. You just laugh at me, it's embarrassing.'

'That's the point, dick-head,' she replied lovingly.

'Right then, you asked for it,' I said.

First Love

When I was eighteen, I went on holiday with my girlfriend. A big thing, a very big thing. Her parents were quite religious — got on with my mother famously — and I was gobsmacked when they said yes to the request. With hindsight I suppose that they thought a ring and marriage was on the cards. We had been going out together for a year and half and in those days that meant a wedding was a done deal.

We had lost our virginity to each other, well I had to her and I assumed, though come to think of it she never said, and maybe that story of her slipping on to a blunt railing spike when she was younger was a cover up.

'Sounds plausible,' Karine said, muffled into my shoulder with what could have been a snigger.

I ignored her.

I had booked a table at the La Mon hotel and she drank too much of the very expensive wine — I think the *maître d'* knew how inexperienced I was and screwed me over.

'Maybe he slipped on to a railing too,' this time there was much more than a snigger from her.

'I give up,' I said, you've started laughing at me already.

'Sher chill out. I love just lying here listening to you talk, I don't mean to keep interrupting but you know I can't keep my gob shut,' she pulled herself tight against me and I couldn't help feeling that her milk swollen dubs were being used as a weapon. 'I'm not being mean, please keep going. I need this so much.'

I lay in silent protest for about five seconds then gave in.

We got back to my parent's house and I managed to get her into the front room. That we were allowed in there unchaperoned was only down to the fact that my mother thought that religious moral fortitude was an inherited trait. I learned that it is exactly the opposite and had used that fact to my benefit many times beforehand.

Being sent away on trips to the Scottish Highlands or Donegal, I always tried to show interest in the seemingly most religious girl in the group. Once the parents and teachers were out of the way, true rebellious nature intervened. Released from that strait-laced, straight-jacket existence they became mad things, lusting after all the delights they of necessity denied themselves at home.

'You skanky little shark, you wee cynical, horny bastard!' Karine said, lifting her head up to look me in the eye.

'Look, young male hormones, bad role models, and a world that looked at woman as objects. I didn't make it. I just lived in it,' I pleaded. 'Took me years to throw of that conditioning. Look at how I treat you?'

'Mmm. I wouldn't say you had a choice in that, but I'll take your point, you're not a cynical horny bastard now,' she said, lying back down.

'Well certainly not all three,' I mumbled.

After my mother's 'Just called in to say hello' security check at the thirty-minute mark things got a bit serious. She took off her underwear and put it beneath her as she lay on the couch and hoicked her skirt up until I had a glimpse of the little furry animal I'd been trying to see for months.

'Mmm really, little furry animal,' came the snort, from somewhere near my neck.

She pulled me down on top of her and told me she was ready. I struggled to get my trousers down while still kissing her but managed and lay between her legs.

I think I must have poked at her perineum about a dozen times before I hit the right place. Chris! What a surprise. It didn't last long but I couldn't help thinking that she should have at least moved a little.

The plan exploded in my head very soon after, the only way to get unfettered access to this wonderous new toy was if we could go somewhere and be on our own for a long period. A holiday no less.

I had to wait nearly a year because there was no way they would allow such a thing while I was underage. But I could book it and dream of it.

The much-anticipated day arrived. We left for Dublin airport waved off by her parents — not sure if the look in her father's eye was relief or hatred — and arrived to find that what we thought would be three hours early was, in fact, one hour too late.

A postal strike in the Irish Republic had left us un-notified of the changes in flight times and we had no idea what to do. The woman at the check-in noted that there was another flight the next day to the same airport, by the same company, and directed us to their desk.

Twenty minutes later we were booked on that flight and now had to find somewhere to spend the night in Dublin that was within our budget.

That was easier said than done. Having driven around seemingly in circles for four hours, it was now dark, and we had come to the conclusion that it would have to be a Bed & Breakfast rather than a hotel, so I pulled into the next one we saw.

The woman at the reception looked at us long and hard. 'One night, ye say. From tha Narth ar yee. Ya doon't look married?'

Foolishly I said that we weren't, not yet.

'Well then, two rooms it'll be.' And proceeded to produce two room keys for rooms at opposite ends of the establishment. There was certainly no fun and games that night.

We hit the airport in plenty of time the next morning and ended up in Pula Airport in sunny Yugoslavia lumped in with a tour group bound for Opatija, which was in the wrong direction. When we got to their hotel and the guide had sorted everyone else out, she came to tell us that she had arranged for a taxi to take us to our hotel in Porec.

Being inexperience travellers, I'm sure that he screwed me over on the fare — I waited for the comment from the woman on my shoulder, but she managed to keep it in that time.

So, we finally arrived at our hotel to begin our holiday, with just enough for a few drinks to enliven the fact that we would need to eat breakfast and dinner in the hotel and do without lunch. Still, we were just in time for last orders in the restaurant, so we dropped our bags and headed in.

These days we're told over and over not to drink the water or eat anything with water on it but not then. Oh no. Not then.

She plunged into a salad and before we'd even finished the one glass of wine, we'd allowed ourselves and lingered over, she was a vivid shade of pale. She rushed off to the toilet and said she'd see me up in the room.

It took about forty minutes before she appeared then disappeared into the bathroom. I was asleep before she came out. I told her that I'd fallen asleep as soon as she arrived to try and spare her blushes. But the memory of the noises in the night cooled any chance of morning ardour.

She seemed well enough to go out and about and we skipped breakfast and sat on the beach most of the day. Back at the hotel in the afternoon our ignorance of the strength of the sun was now apparent. I was suffering from burnt skin on my face, shoulders, chest and back. She however, was suffering from sun stroke.

I tried to keep her cool but the water I got for her didn't help and so we spent the next three days stuck in the room in the dark. After that I'd had enough, I needed to escape that hell of sound and smell and bailed out and left her for a few hours a day when she was asleep. I wandered the beach and enjoyed the scents wafting from every restaurant and looked at the happy couples with envy bordering on hatred.

She was still weak when we got back on the plane home and I'm ashamed to say that I stopped going out with her shortly thereafter — I'd discovered the joys that motorcycling had to bring. Her parents cut me dead whenever they saw me, I'm not sure why, she must have told them that she didn't have a good time.

'Poor little Sheriff. No action all week from your grubby little plan,' she said, leaning up on her elbow.

'Yep. Not a Whee or a Squeak or a Hoohah,' I said sadly.

'That poor girl. You monster. You probably scarred her for life,' and she poked me in the ribs with her fist. 'God my boobs hurt.'

'She became a WAG and married some prominent Linfield guy, probably happily ever after, and what do you mean hurt?' I said a bit worried.

'I bet they never went on holiday to Yugoslavia,' she replied. 'They're too full. I need the baby to wake up.'

'Oh! Fuck no,' I most supportively said.

Tell me something to keep your mind off it, how about the Falklands?

'Jesus Sher,' What. Now?

HMS *Ardent*

She was supposed to join the *Canberra*, which was acting as a troop carrier, but her little group of a doctor, three nurses and three orderlies was delayed by a train problem and so were temporary attached to HMS *Ardent* for the trip to the Falklands. The *Ardent* sailed a little later with some other ships but eventually caught up with the fleet in the South Atlantic. They were meant to transfer across using some modern type of Breeches buoy, but the weather was appalling, and it was judged too dangerous.

Even when there were no storms the seas were colossal, the ships going up those huge waves and down into the canyons of the troughs with the white-water flooding over the decks looked like little helpless grey specks in the immensity of ocean.

She felt sorry for all the landlubber squaddies stacked like frankfurters in every available space throughout the task force ships. In the beginning they were all Yeehaw! Roller coaster time. Fun for the first few days. Then came the cold merciless realisation that it wasn't going to end. They were not going to be able to stop and get off the never-ending rise and fall and twist and sway, and it became agony. Thrown about with the pitch and yaw, slammed into the steel doors and bulkheads, unable to even walk to the head in safety to retch endlessly, they hung on in those grimmest of circumstances to the security of their stinking wretched bunks.

Her friends looked on her with envy, when they could do

anything other than lean over the rail or the rim of the toilet bowl. She took to the movement of the ship like one born to it and it threw her back to the many trips with her beloved Anu on the wild Irish sea in skiffs no bigger than a large plank.

She imagined the ocean laughing at these tiny things crawling on its skin, so fragile that even the unleashing of the smallest amount of its power destroyed them. They were as nothing, only the noise they made stood them out in the vastness. The harsh clanking and clinking of the metal, the booming and the whooshing of the engines and the all too faint cries of despair that often followed them into the depths.

The ocean just played with them, like an otter with a seashell, tossing the ship around like it was weightless. Then jangling all their nerves and throwing them about like chaff to the wind as without warning they would hit a wave and practically stop. Three thousand tons of steel hitting a brick wall, it was terrifying.

Apart from them — the green army rats — the rest of the HMS *Ardent's* compliment were experienced sailors. Just as well, as the other six in her group produced enough sick to fill bathtubs. She shook her head in dismay at the thought of what must be prevalent on the troop ships with their floods of vomit swamping the decks.

But this was a ship of war, at war, and the misery and discomfort had to be put aside as the captain insisted that both port and starboard watches be fully manned. Karine and one of the orderlies covered the dog watches and first watch and as soon as this was over at midnight, she'd hit the protection and comfort of her bunk and sleep, trying to ignore the smell and constant gagging of her companions. The doctor rotated things with the ship's medical officer to provide continuous cover but more than once Karine extended her watch to let the others rest.

It wasn't as if there was much to do however, the odd bruise or cut and one broken arm was the sum of it on the trip out, but they trained hard, learning the way of the ship in various action conditions, finding their stations in the dark and staying out of the way of the damage control parties during drills.

A month or so after leaving Devonport she had her first look of the islands, the crew acknowledged that she was an old hand, balancing easily in the swells and riding the yaw and pitch like an expert, and were tolerant of her on the deck or occasionally the bridge. And then the *Ardent* arrived in Falkland Sound and the ship alarms went off and the call went out over the PA for Action Stations.

Her medical team had been assigned station in the dining hall and as Karine rushed down the gangway from the deck, she heard the Anti-Aircraft guns start. The noise! That hammering clanging noise, it was like being in a steel drum while someone hits it over and over with a crowbar a hundred times a minute, and that was from two decks down.

It was over almost as soon as it started and the news filtered down to them that the bombs had missed, falling on each side of the ship and failing to explode. As she was returning to her bunk, trying to come to terms with what that meant, that someone was deliberately dropping explosives in the hope of killing her, the PA called Action Stations again and there was no more time to think. She ran back to the dining hall to join the others and the guns started again.

The worst thing was not being able to see anything, all she had was a small round view from a porthole, glimpses of the sea and occasionally another ship in the distance. She felt for those in the bowels of the ship with nothing but steel walls on their horizon.

There was a huge clashing bang and the ship seemed for a moment to stand on its bow then come crashing down. The fire alarms went off and the PA was calling for damage-control teams to the Hanger deck.

There was nothing to do but to pick herself up and wait, and a few minutes later the first casualties were brought in.

Although this was her first tour, she had seen some injuries before, from training exercises and general wounds and damage from car accidents and so on when she did duties at the hospital, but nothing prepared her for this. Not in her worst nightmares could she have imagined this.

First there was the smell. The injured were brought in and piled on the mess tables, and the smell hit her, a miasmic cloud somehow attached to the men. The cordite, and something like marzipan from the explosives, and the fuel oil. But worst of all the burnt flesh, and the exposed organs and bones, then the shit and the blood and there were so many of them.

The ship was manoeuvring from side to side in vicious sweeps and she was constantly falling, slipping in the mess spilled to the floor from the insides of human beings as she was thrown around. The AA guns were going relentlessly and even the big gun would occasionally add its bass roar to things.

Her feet went out from under her and just as she looked up the most perfect round holes appeared in the side of the ship followed immediately by a sickening wet, slapping noise as the canon rounds swept the orderlies and tore them apart along with the injured sailor they were carrying. Then more bombs exploded, and she had a glimpse of the huge steel bulkheads bending and breaking and then the lights went out.

The fire suppression system came on, and the emergency

lighting system. The smell of smoke was very strong but quickly blown away as the wind howled in from the far end of the hall that had disappeared into a pile of twisted and blackened steel.

Karine and a fellow nurse grabbed the injured and carrying them one at a time made their way to the front of the ship where they piled them on the deck side by side. They went running back and forth until they had retrieved them all, leaving the dead until last. Other hands were helping and bringing the injured and dead from other parts of the ship and then they all waited in the freezing air for help.

The ship's engines had stopped, and they drifted with the wind which would occasionally blow from the stern of the ship, bringing acinic fumes from the massive clouds of black smoke at the rear into their noses and eyes, swamping and choking them. By this time, the ship was listing quite badly but she could see another huge grey shape slowly approaching through the smoke.

Eventually a gangway was secured at the front and she heard the PA announce, Abandon Ship. She was shivering with the cold and shock as she stumbled along this narrow bridge to safety but the man in front of her was moving quite slowly and she could see blood running down his uniform bottoms from under his T-shirt. Both his arms were in slings and as she moved closer to help him, a swell twisted the gangplank and he fell and rolled under the safety rail into the sea. She didn't know what she was thinking, maybe that he'd suffered enough but she couldn't just let him go and jumped over the rail after him.

It was to her great good fortune that the swell was running in the right direction and it pushed her and the seaman clear of the bows of the *Ardent* into the open choppy water of Grantham Sound. Had it been running in the opposite direction they would have been swept into the burning maelstrom at the rear of the ship.

She swam to the man and took him around the chin and lay back into the waves telling him to keep kicking and that help was on its way. For one terrible moment she thought that maybe no one had seen them fall and that no one was coming and that they would drown. She could see land to the north and south, but it was way too far to reach.

As it was, she was near her end by the time the ship's RIB got to them, the cold had sapped her strength and she was fading in and out nearing unconsciousness and the deep dark that would result.

She vaguely remembers being hauled into the boat and a blanket laid around her shoulders, but vividly remembers the seaman being hauled into the boat and a blanket laid over his head.

'Oh! Babe, I'm so sorry,' and I pulled her close. I held her tight but after a few minutes she pushed away from me, her eyes were slightly puffy but dry.

'Sher, I'm in agony, wake her up,' she said grimacing.

'No, let's not. She could get used to this longer sleep and that will be great for you in the long run, hang on, please,' I pleaded.

'I can't hold on.'

'I may get a slap in the ear for this, but… I could help,' I suggested, tentatively.

No hand flew out to smack me, 'You wouldn't mind?'

'No, not at all,' I said softly, frightened to disturb the possibility.

She rolled away from me a bit and unbuttoned her pyjama top and took it off, she then wriggled up on to the pillow and reached down and unclipped her maternity bra, exposing her very milk full breasts. I rolled on my side and looked into her eyes and then slowly slid my head down to her left nipple.

As soon as I touched it a jet of warm, very sweet and smooth liquid hit my mouth, it was surprisingly erotic, but tasted nothing like normal milk, and I suckled a bit more.

'Holy fucking Christ!' I heard her say, 'How long has it been?'

'Six weeks,' I said, and moved to the right.

She raised her bum of the mattress and slid her pants off, 'Holy fucking Christ!

A short time later I was lying beside her watching her re-clip her bra, 'Congratulations,' she said, now I've got a sore hole and sore tits.' But she smiled as she said it. 'Actually, now that I know that you will, I can call on you to do that again when needed.'

'Happy to help,' I said and rolled on to my back, maybe these months to come will have an upside.

The doorbell rang and woke the baby. I got out of bed and looked through the window of our bathroom that allowed me to see the doorway.

'It's some man in a suit with a briefcase, I'll go and see what he wants.

The Convent

I had a short but sweet — by my standards — visit to hospital where a kindly and cute doctor told me she'd never seen a medical history like mine before. She wondered if perhaps I'd just taken on a new job as a stuntman but was shit at it. I didn't have the strength for a riposte and allowed her to book me in for a few days R&R as she called it.

I lay awake at first, the events of the previous night cycling through my mind over and over again. One minute elated at having survived such a cold attempt to kill me, the next almost comatose with guilt and remorse at having killed.

It seemed so everyday, and ordinary to them, the taking of life, my life. I think that was the most appalling thing — I was a nobody just like he warned me. In the end it just happened so fast, like I was rubbish to be taken out, a small squeamish job to be gotten over with quickly and efficiently.

I kept playing the last few moments in my head and it left me wondering and imagining. Where was the uplifting background music? Where the adagio in strings? Where the empathy provoking operatic messiah as I lay wounded in the muck and about to die. It didn't seem right to have a few meaty smacks and some groaning as a backing track.

I'd dragged myself out of that alleyway, bruised, bloody and broken and hailed a cab in my sodden clothes. I was most grateful to him for stopping in the first place and risking the fare but even more grateful to him for dropping me at A & E when I clapped out on the back seat unconscious.

Thankfully, I eventually slept and if I awoke screaming in the night, I was unaware of it. The looks on the nurses' faces at morning rounds suggested that I had, and I found myself uncomfortable with their pity. The urge to leave was tempered with exhaustion but the IVs of broad-spectrum antibiotics, steroids and fluids soon had me chomping at the bit.

The same doctor discharged me after I told her that I'd a new gig to get to, standing in for Val Kilmer who was afraid of heights. She told me to take care of myself with a wry smile and added that I was better looking than him anyway. I waited for the rise and sarky comment from Karine in my head, but she was gone, and swamped with grief I hid my face while fussing with my jacket.

Fretting with the dressings wrapping my chest, I barely heard the taxi driver going on about that morning's wonderful visit from the new pope. About how he had travelled the length and breadth of the city in his bespoke pope-tractor-trailer. How screaming crowds had packed the streets on the off chance that they might be caught in the sweep of his incessant Papal blessing.

He might have asked the crowds to take their rubbish and empties home with them I almost said, but the vast number of crucifixes dangling from the driver's rear-view mirror made me bite my tongue. Instead, I mumbled something innocuous and vaguely agreeable.

He dumped me at my door still ranting about the visitation. I paid him, got out, and then slammed the car door as loudly as I could in the middle of his blurb. Petty yes, but it gave me a little lift.

I just about managed to keep from popping the pills the doc gave me until I'd made it to my kitchen sink.

Was I done?

I sank down with my back to the wall, nursing my stump and breathing as shallowly as I could to stop my chest hurting and closed my eyes and fell into an exhausted sleep.

I had a wonderful dream where I was having a terrific screaming fight with Karine that led to a bit of pushing and tugging, some risqué wrestling and then some passionate make-up, but the only crystal-clear thing that I remembered when I awoke was, 'What else are you going to do?'

I gave myself two days to regain my strength, such as it was, and to let my more minor wounds heal a bit. Then I grabbed the phone book and started. Manipulating things with one hand was becoming easier but every so often I'd forget, and curse as I banged the stump of my left wrist against something that I meant to pick up.

I was surprised at the great number of places in the greater Belfast area that you might find a nun. Schools to convents to care homes to parochial houses to name a few. I was acting as a wayward next of kin hinting at a legacy and in two days had worked my way through all the Sister Concetta's I could find. Eliminating the Concetta-Marie's had left me with two Concetta-Patricia's, and I was on my way to a convent that I knew well after hearing that the other nun was Spanish and on her death bed.

A little frisson of something worked its way up my spine as I entered the gates of the convent and spotted the prefab buildings of the youth club in the corner of the car park. I was a bit surprised that it was still going but I suppose no connection to my brother's murder ever stuck. Anyway, must be ancient history to those now in attendance.

The buildings were red brick, highlighted at the edges with pale sandstone. The same sandstone was used for the window frames, small and large, and to outline the roof edges and door frames. It all struck me as classy and timeless and, of course, expensive.

A young acolyte met me at the huge front door, and I admired the gothic columns, made from the same pale sandstone, the wide luxuriously carpeted corridors and the equally wide marble staircase with its gilded balusters and newel posts. Everywhere the Virgin Mary looked down on us and if not her, then many a saint in their alcove as we passed. As always, I was struck by the lack of God and the ubiquity of humans worshipped in such places.

She opened a plain, white-glossed door into what appeared to be a small chapel. At the centre rear of the room was a small altar complete with red velvet kneeler under a high stained-glass window depicting a female saint-martyr in chains beneath the claws of a lion. Her angelic face and hands-at-prayer seemed to be made of nacre, such was the multihued light reflecting from them. The floor was black and white mosaic tiles, perfectly clean, and all the walls were brick, freshly whitewashed.

'Sister Concetta-Patricia will be with you shortly,' she said, ushering me in and closing the door.

I was shocked at how cold it was, but I supposed the sisters were not given to luxury anywhere beyond the spaces that they shared with the diocesan's offices. More than ten minutes on my knees in here and I'd be off to the refectory for some hot cocoa and a warm bacon bap. Life serving the Lord Jesus can go too far with this deprivation and suffering lark if you ask me. I could understand austere or minimal conditions to focus the mind but why would the God of the Christians want you to suffer while you were praising or beseeching him?

I walked towards the small window to look at the glass and

was surprised by what seemed to be the bare bosom of the young woman. Just as I craned my neck for a better look, the door opened behind me and I turned to see a very large nun enter. I took a step towards her and held out my hand.

'Thank you for seeing me sis… Fuck me bendy!' I exclaimed at the end. For as I had stepped closer the nun had raised her head and I saw her eyes. Eyes that I would never forget. Eyes that I had last seen in my kitchen laughing at me as a trigger was pulled and a love extinguished. Eyes that had been dead to my pleas and saw a child condemned.

'What! Whaaah!' was all I could manage as two huge fat hands wrapped around my neck, lifted me off the ground and slammed me into the wall.

Crystal clear ice-chip blue eyes drilled into mine while through her compressed lips she hissed incomprehensible rage noises at me. I tried to kick out while grabbing her hand and pulling, but the ponderous dugs, huge belly and morbid mass held me against the bricks. Realising I had no leverage, I tried thumping her around the head, but she simply ducked between her outstretched arms and carried on squeezing while my fist bounced, ineffectually, off the back and sides of her skull.

Being strangled doesn't actually feel that bad at the beginning. You have enough air in your lungs for a minute or so and apart from the pain of having your neck crushed there is only the dread of what's to come. Very quickly however, that takes precedence as your body realises that it can't breathe. You start to struggle, grabbing at the constriction on your neck, but all to no avail as your need to exhale becomes mortal and the deep dark closes in, and your efforts to escape become increasingly feeble and futile.

I was looking into that dark and fought to gather enough

fluid in my mouth to spit my last defiance into her face. I forced my eyes to focus on hers, glinting through the mass of red flesh and bulging, engorged veins running from the corner of her wimple across her forehead and temples, and a strange thing happened.

There was a flush of blood into her left eye as if someone had injected it into her sclera and as it spread into a little river system flooding the cornea, she gave a small, constrained moan, dropped me and collapsed onto her knees. I slid the short distance down the wall to my feet and was raising my hand to my neck when she fell forward and head-butted me in the balls.

What better time to join the millions of happy, clappy people secure in their shared delusion or faith — depending on how you view it. A venerated religious site long used by the Holy Sisters and an act of God, a verifiable miracle that saves my worthless hide. Surely, that would have me on my knees begging for forgiveness and pledging my life to Jesus.

Instead, I was thankful for the poor nutrition and lack of exercise that had bought me my life. I forced my way from under her limp mass and let her head fall with a nice meaty clunk, unencumbered by my gonads, to hit the whitewashed wall. Then fell to my knees moaning 'Jesus,' while throwing up on to the back of her dead neck from the sickening pain in my testicles.

The House

A couple of days later the doorbell rang, it was a week or so before Christmas, and I opened it to find Chief Inspector John-Henry McCracken on my step. I invited him in and noted him noticing my suitcases sitting in the hall.

'Going somewhere?' he asked. Nosey fucker, I thought.

'Mmm, would you like some coffee?' I said, ignoring his question and led the way into the kitchen. He sat on her seat, but I said nothing, pouring from a cafetiere into a mug that I took from under the island and clinking it down on the marble surface.

'I wanted a chat with you about a few things and to confirm our position with respect to others,' he said. 'I'm happy to do this at the station if you prefer, but I thought you might be a bit more comfortable at home, given your recent experiences.'

'That's most kind,' I replied, but he was oblivious to the sarcastic tone. 'Not off for the holidays with Mrs Chief Inspector McCracken and all the baby McCrackens.

'I'd rather keep things professional. If that's all right,' he said.

He cleared his throat. 'Item. The alleged killing of an individual known to you as 'Rarebit' at the Sailor's Rest pub on the late evening of the 11th of December,' he started, in what was undoubtedly his official voice.

'After thorough investigation, interrogation of the indigenous population, document research and door-to-door questioning, we can find no record of any such individual, living

216

or deceased. The official conclusion is that the whole affair was imagined, brought on by previous head injury and that file has been closed.' He looked down at his mug and paused to take a sip.

I was taken aback for a moment, open mouthed, then set for a rejoinder, but he rushed on.

'Item. Complaints of assault resulting in grievous bodily harm by persons known as Rarebit and Wolfgang at the instigation of one Jessie, in the grounds and surrounds of the aforesaid public house.' Again, he paused for a sip. 'No further action will be taken as there is insufficient evidence to bring a successful prosecution.'

I got in quickly this time. 'Fuck me! Are you telling me that scumbag is going to walk away from all this? I knew it! I fucking knew it! He said as much you know. That all you RUC and establishment type fuckwits were in his pocket.'

An indignant CI put a little gravitas into his voice, 'I'm in no fucker's pocket, son and I don't want to ever hear you say that again,' he gathered himself with another little sip. 'Look that greaser toe-rag is going to get his sooner or later anyway. Maybe you can't have justice directly, but you can smile when you read of him falling into a compactor or some such. Normally I'd help that situation with a well-placed size fourteen, but I've been warned off big time.' He paused for a few moments and looked around the room.

'This is a very beautiful room, very peaceful and calm, your wife had good taste,' he thought for a moment, 'Very centred.'

Jesus Christ! Had he come here straight from the dentists and a three-week-old copy of *Home and Hounds* magazine.

I had to swallow a little before I could respond and all I could manage was, 'Yes she did.'

'Right then', he continued in the same direct succinct manner. 'Item. Death of Sister Concetta-Patricia Louise Maguire at the Sisters of Mercy House on the evening of the 14th of December. The pathologist has had a good dig around in her bits and decided natural causes — haemorrhagic stroke. Massive apparently. Shut her down quickly and completely — luckily for you I'd say. Case closed.'

I had to exercise all my control so as not to shout in his face, 'What! You're kidding me. How can that be case closed? What about my wife and the sister, surely, you're launching further investigations into what went on there?'

'My colleague Chief Inspector Mullan is handling that case and he will, no doubt, be in touch to give you all the necessary info. but in short…' he took a longer sip, perhaps to fortify himself, 'Your wife's case is closed as well. The theory is that for reason or reasons unknown the good sister shot your wife and indirectly caused the death of your baby girl. Nun's dead now. case closed.'

I couldn't believe this. No investigation, no follow-up, no answers! I cradled my forehead with my hand, elbow on the marble surface, 'This can't be right,' I pleaded.

'Look son. Times are what they are. Resources are finite and even if I was inclined to look at this further, I can't. Orders. And let me tell you that this isn't the movies. I can't go rogue, break all procedures and stomp over everyone just to solve the case at the eleventh hour and be forgiven. I would end-up in the Crum' and dead by the end of the day. I've put far too many of those slimy fuck-rats in there.'

'This can't be right,' I said again, slumping on the counter, with my chin now in the crook of my arm, 'Everything I've been through. Do you think this is right?'

He thought for a while, 'I'm going to tell you a story, that's all it is and all it will ever be. Okay?'

I lifted my head and nodded.

'Imagine a church run foster home or orphanage full of fearful and abandoned young girls guarded by a coven of nuns. Imagine that overall control of this house resides in a priest who unlike many of his fellows has a taste for females. Young, just approaching puberty seems to be his thing.

With or without the connivance of the sisters he gives private lessons to these young girls, persuading them into sex acts by suggesting that they are doing God's work. Many will have been destroyed by his attentions, but not all. Further imagine a young girl, bigger than most, perhaps not as attractive, who yearns for attention. It doesn't matter that the others tell her horror stories of their time with the Father, she just wants to be picked, to be noticed. Finally, her time comes, and somehow instead of being hurt and destroyed, she accepts whatever spiel he puts out to justify his rapes.

In the end, she not only accepts it, but welcomes it, comes to worship him. Perhaps she deludes herself that she is in love, but from that time on she is a willingly participant and faithful servant. She follows his career, his meteoric rise to bishop, to archbishop, to cardinal and finally all the way to that chair in Rome as the biggest Christ worshipping honcho of all.

As she realises her Love will become the master of the church throughout the world, she conceives a great task to protect him from the possibility of girl ghosts of the past rising up to defame him or, as she sees it, betray him. God has selected her Love as Pope and as his faithful servant by God's will, she must act to preserve him from the cruel lies that those unworthy of his affection might spread.

Every girl that may be a danger to him must be killed,' he pauses again to finish his coffee.

I was sitting up again hanging on his every word, 'Did he know? Did he somehow communicate with her or lead her to believe that this was his wish? Did he manipulate her into this in some way?' I asked.

'We have no way of knowing, but it is possible. Obviously, his distance insulates him from all this anyway,' he then added, somewhat bitterly I thought, 'No investigation into him will ever be sanctioned.'

I couldn't take this, 'How many?' I asked, 'How many did she kill? Was Karine the first?'

'We don't know for sure and may never know,' he said, looking down at his mug, perhaps in shame or guilt, 'but seven that I am aware of in the North and maybe a further five or six in the South. And no, it looks like your wife was the last.'

'It's him,' I said, for some reason growling in my throat. 'He is the proximal cause and it's he who should pay the price.'

'I can't say I disagree, son,' he replied, 'but that's not how the world works.'

'It's how the God-fucking world should work,' there was still a hint of a snarl in my voice.

'Why did you set me on Jessie's path?'

He looked a little off-step for a brief moment but covered it up quickly, 'I can't say that I did. I simply answered your question if I remember correctly.'

'Come on. For fuck's sake you owe me,' I pushed a little.

He looked around the kitchen again for a minute and I waited him out.

'Not sure I owe you, son, but for what it's worth,' he started. 'Pretend I had a slimy superior officer who, like all his kind, look for that one case that can make their career. A juicy scandal with political overtones that can propel our boy wonder into the media spotlight and fast advancement all the way to the top. Well, mine got a hold of my notes on the murder of a few young women — mostly ignored it must be said — and then demanded to know my thoughts and suspicions and my half-baked conclusions.

These women were down-and-outs, or druggies or low-rent prostitutes, and after he forced me to provide him with all my information, I could see the gleam in his eye and a sort of yearning avarice leak out of his snake like skin.

His problem of course was that any investigation into our cardinal, almost certain to be promoted pontiff would have meant his end too, and he couldn't order me to investigate because of the stop order from on high.

When your wife was killed, he called me into his office almost as soon as I'd got back from dragging you out of the supermarket. He was practically foaming at the mouth with the chance that gave him, and he ordered me to get you involved hoping, I suppose, that by exposing the link he could obliquely get at the priestly wonder, become the golden boy and fulfil all his wanky dreams.'

He cradled his empty mug and managed to look a little sheepish, I thought.

'So, you were just following orders,' I said softly, and watched as his eyes narrowed and a little shudder raced across his face. 'Excuse me a moment.' I walked past him dragging the stump of my left wrist slowly across the marble surface and when sure he was watching, rubbed at the bruises on my neck with my hand and went to the downstairs loo.

'More coffee?' I said when I returned. 'Still hard as fuck to do the simplest things with one hand.'

'Ahh. No thanks. Best get going,' he replied. I ignored him and poured a refill from the cafetiere. He looked at me for a few moments and then picked the mug up and sipped.

'My father built this house.' I said, moving my stool away with my hip and gesturing around with my hand. 'I mean he actually built it with his own hands. Okay, he had a bit of help putting the roof trestles on, but apart from that he did everything himself. It took him the best part of twenty years. Spare hours here and there, holidays and weekends. Teaching himself how to plaster and plumb, how to wire electrics and lay bricks.

I always assumed that he did it to get away from my mother, not that I could blame him. But we had holidays away as a family and he was always on the side-lines at Saturday games for my brother and me. So, it wasn't as if he was neglecting us to get it done.

Isn't it strange how memory works? Up until very recently I had believed that he spent all his spare time here and it was all so that he could leave my mother and live a peaceful life with grace and quiet in his twilight years once we had flown the nest. The thing is, my brother is long dead, and I have been gone from the nest for years, and he deliberately left the kitchen undone! The heart of any house and the space that most women, wives, would want the most input in.

I know he was happy here. He would bring me sometimes when he felt like just wandering his small wood on the East side. Hunting he'd say. Let's get up early and go hunting. I just assumed he was allowed on some farmer's land.

He could never bring himself to shoot anything living, never again. I mean, this is a man that helped spiders from the bath and opened windows to let flies and wasps out. He just liked the idea of it and carrying his old under and over Beretta shotgun around

222

pretending to be the lord of the manor. Many hundreds of shotgun cartridges expended but not a single animal harmed was the style.

I liked that and was so very much like him. A gentle person, you know. I have never knowingly hurt another person. I have never started any fight, even as a child. I've never bullied anyone. In fact, my first response in any situation is towards de-escalation, towards peace.' I paused and watched him finish his coffee and set his mug down.

'A wimp, you'd say. A coward too, no doubt. But that's all right. It doesn't matter, because she loved me for it. She loved me because I was gentle and would never harm her. All the shite that she suffered in her life, all the abuse and violence could be left where it belonged. Wrapped up tightly and stored in the past. She could be herself and relax and think herself safe.' I was crying a little now and wasn't sure if he was looking at me with contempt or pity.

I took a breath to steady myself and leaned on the counter to look directly at him.

'But you changed me!' the soft growl was back in my throat. 'You threw me into the fire and called it orders. And although I accepted it as just a complicated way to commit suicide, I was instead annealed, melded and reformed, forged into something else. I have been broken — face, jaw and chest — humiliated, tortured and maimed and set-up for death like I was a lamb at slaughter. And I have killed! Because of you! Who pays for that!' I shouted.

He started out of his seat and held his hands up placatingly, 'Woah, son take it easy. It's not like I could have known, is it?'

And that moment decided it for me definitively, 'Known? Of course, you knew. And you should be ashamed,' I said softly, looking down.

I raised my head after a moment, caught his eye and nodded at my suitcases, 'Anyway I'm off.' He turned to follow my gaze and as he did so, I bent down and lifted my father's shotgun off the shelf of the island. He no doubt saw something in his peripheral vision and snapped his head back around, but it was too late. Supporting the barrel on my left stump I squeezed the trigger and blew his left hand off. He squealed in agony and as I stepped around the island to stand over him, he let go of his mangled wrist and the remnants of his palm and went for his revolver.

'No!' I shouted, 'Stop right there. Don't make me fire the other barrel.'

'You stupid little fucker, you've fucked my hand and I'm going to see you rammed for it,' he hissed through his teeth and the pain.

'Lift your gun out slowly and throw it away,' I ordered. 'Do it and I'll help you, otherwise I'm gone.'

He clicked the holster safety clip off with his thumb and slowly eased his revolver out and slid it across the tabletop. I have no doubt that he could have drawn it fast and shot me before I'd realised what was happening, indeed just that thought often forms one of the many nightmares that wake me each night. I can't be sure why he didn't, maybe I'd pushed the guilt just enough. I'll never know.

I set the shotgun down and grabbed a tea towel and together we got it wrapped around his wrist and pulled it tight. I took the extension phone off the cradle and put it in his hand, pale like the rest of him with shock.

'I have to go now,' I said. 'Need time to get my ticket changed at the airport. Send them after me if you want to.'

'Don't you doubt it. You scabby little fucker. I'll have you in the 'H' blocks before I'm through. You'll be getting done in the arse by all those fairy Red Hand Commandos of Jonny "I'm really a girl" Adair's before the week's out.'

Not sure why but I didn't believe him.

'Where do you think you are going anyway, you wee cunt?'

'Rome,' I said.

Printed in Great Britain
by Amazon

17583689R00130